The Ganymeade Protocol
Don Elwell

Wild Shore Press
2008

The Ganymeade Protocol
by Don Elwell
Copyright 2008
All Rights Reserved

This is a work of fiction and philosophy, and should be regarded as such. Any direct references to persons, places, things or to elements your own life are in your own mind, not in this text.

Wild Shore Press is a publisher of fine literature, philosophy, poetry, science fiction, plays, and many other amazing things. You may find us on the web at:

WWW. WildShorePress.com

The Ganymeade Protocol

A novel by Don Elwell

Kate

She had been very very careful to do nothing at all
unusual, nothing out of character all week long. She had
made sure that all her homework was done, that she
studied for the quiz, that she raised no "interesting"
questions in her Morals and Futures class. . . .she had
been, in short, what she was supposed to be: the
perfect daughter, the perfect student, the perfect
little future citizen of that most perfect of all nations,
America.

She didn't dare even look at Sandy, for fear someone
might catch on. They'd been planning this for months,
years maybe. They had everything in place. They had
gotten appropriate signatures and thumbprints on all
the appropriate documents to excuse their absence by
shuffling the forms in with other of the school's
interminable legal paperwork that was sent home for
parental approval. They had, slowly, ever so slowly,
secreted away food, clothing, personal effects. . . .

But for right now, they were perfect. They had even carefully maintained their flaws. Sandy still insisted on wearing black at all times, a "phase" derided by her mother as being like "that satanic goth stuff when I was a girl". Kate had kept her readings of "questionable" materials, histories and gnostica not approved by the public schools and the state church. Tiny flaws, like beauty marks, to set into contrast the otherwise perfect children of the perfect nation.

Except.

Except late at night, when Kate would wind up the old shortwave receiver left by her late father, would put in the ear buds and listen. Listen to a blank space on the dial, hissing with static and government jamming and electrical noise, listening to a space where no signal should be, a frequency her father had shown her long ago before the cancer had eaten him.

Listening, and falling asleep to the hiss and the silence.

Except tonight.

Except tonight was different. Tonight, something had pried her out of her sleep at 2 AM. Something. A snatch of rhythm. A sound where there should be no sound. She listened, scarcely breathing. The bits and pieces became a beat, some shattered rendering of a caribbean melody. The signal faded. Then it was there again. Some woman singing in Spanish. Not Spanish. Portuguese. Then some rock thing in French, the signal gaining clarity with each passing moment. Then something odd and Celtic, haunting. A melange of cultures and music. Then a far too long silence. Then a voice that simply said "you are listening to the voice of the fleet."

Katie's phone chimed instantly. She didn't even need to look. She picked it up, thumbed it on, and said "I heard."

"Just making sure." Sandy's voice on the other end.
Her voice was shaking.

"See you in the morning."

Kate curled up in her covers, curled up in the music, a voice from the world outside. She drifted with it, dreaming. She sailed with her father, hearing stories remembered and half remembered. She danced through warm water and warm days when the world was kinder, while, somewhere out on the horizon, hope was tacking its uneven course--with any luck--in her direction.

When she awoke, the radio had wound itself down and the cheesy alarm was buzzing the bible verse of the day incomprehensibly at her bedside. She returned the radio to its hiding place, along with the other Things She Did Not Have. It was going to be an interesting day.

2: On the History of the Fleet

Most people, even today, fail to realize that the history of the Fleet reaches back so far, or is so profoundly tied with the events of the 19th and 20th centuries as well as those of our own.

So here is a brief story of the Fleet's beginnings. As our current Admiral is fond of saying, some if it may even be true.

The story begins around the turn of the Nineteenth Century, just after the war of 1812, and it begins with a young British Officer named William Augustus Bowles. Bowles, born in Maryland in the New World, had served the Crown well through their losing cause in the Americas, having been both soldier and spy for British forces fighting the American Insurrection. Following the war, this James Bondish character is captured by Spain, jumps overboard off the Canaries, swims miles through shark infested waters, walks 140 miles overland to a British outpost, and begins a series of outlandish and utterly romantic episodes until stationed in the doomed British outpost in Pensacola where, to make a long story less complex, he was tricked by a jealous Commanding

Officer, court-martialed, stripped of rank, and banished to the surrounding swamps.

Had William Bowles been a less resourceful individual, or less of an overachiever, the story might've ended here, but Bowles survived. He was befriended by a Muskogee Chieftain sympathetic to the British (the Muskogee apparently first thought he was the chain man for a South Carolinian survey team, which would have gotten him killed), and became a member of the tribe. The changes he made in Muskogee society were substantial, as were the things he learned from them. Blending their ways with British technology, he improved their agriculture and drilled their warriors into crack troops. Bowles and his Indian soldiers accounted themselves well at the disastrous siege of Pensacola by overwhelming Spanish forces, which earned him a return of his rank in the British army. He was not, however, content to stop there.

Bowles welded together an alliance of Muskogee and Miccusuccee tribes to face the increasing land-grabbing of the Spanish and Americans. Declaring the State of Muskogee to be a national entity, his forces drove the Spanish from their fort in St. Marks. He armed a naval force to patrol the coast against Spanish raids and issued Letters of Marque to privateers preying on Spanish vessels. The British and French, delighted, recognized Muskogee, the British even gifting the new nation with a flag of "mixed British and Indian Colours" to serve as their ensign. Bowles toured Europe as a Muskogee "War Chief" in romanticized Indian garb, eating up all of it. Ultimately, Muskogee claimed land and allegiance as far north as the Tennessee river, with the democratic participation of most of the tribes of the region.

It was that participation that was to be his downfall.

The Spanish offered the confederation a peace treaty of very favorable terms, the only catch was this: The Indians would have to deliver Bowles to Spanish forces as a token of their goodwill. Whereas a year or so earlier this would've been unthinkable, the confederacy had expanded far beyond its original NorthWest Florida tribes. The more numerous Miccusuccee members of the coalition wanted the Spanish as a buffer to American expansion. They simply outvoted the Muskogee loyal to Bowles.

Bowles was jailed in Cuba, where, in ill health, he starved himself to death rather than to "sink so low as to ever speak to a Cuban general." His legacy, distorted over the years and confused by a number of Seminole chiefs taking his name, remains as a pirate legend in the Ft. Walton Beach area of Florida that once may have been his seat of power. So there the story ends.....

......almost.....

Under Bowles' command, though certainly not of his inner circle, was a young American deserter named Jonathan Foote. Foote worshipped Bowles with an admiration that some of his contemporaries termed "unnatural." It is said that when Bowles was handed over to the Spanish, Foote went into a rage that took ten of his Indian brethren to subdue. His bitterness and desire for revenge were so strong that they resulted in his being expelled from the tribe.

Foote and a handful of followers still loyal to their captive commander took one of the Muskogee war canoes (not, by any means, a small vessel), armed with small arms and a carronade, and headed South along the Florida coast. They raided the outskirts of Key West for supplies, and set out for Cuba, with ideas of staging a dramatic raid to rescue Bowles. Sadly, this was not to be.

Foul weather forced the canoe, a vessel ill-suited for rough open water, to the East, where it ultimately grounded on a bar at the edge of the Cay Sal Bank, a broad expanse of shallows and volatile islands formed by the Florida and Cuban currents. Dazed, Foote dragged his followers and their possessions across the shallows to a small island, there to wait out the storm.

The Islands formed by the south eddies of the Gulf stream tend to be elliptical, low, and short lived. Only the largest and most stable, generally anchored by a tangle of mangrove or chunks of coral and limestone, can weather a major storm. Large, in this case, is a relative term. The island on which Foote and his people found themselves was a tidy knoll of mangrove some seven acres square, with the highest point some four feet above mene high tide.

The origin of the island's name "Perrin Island" is in dispute. The most credited account holds that the island collected, as is common in the area, around an obstruction, that obstruction being the ill-fated catboat *Edgar Perrin* which swamped in heavy air on a trip from Grand Cayman to Key West. Other sources contend that the *Perrin* actually went down in Biscayne Bay and that the name is, in fact, a corruption of "Parrot Island." Whatever the source, this was the lump of sand on which Foote and some nineteen survivors found themselves.

The morning brought more grim news. The 40-foot canoe had been smashed to bits on the brain coral of the shallow bottom. Still, they had the small sailing dinghy they had brought with them, their provisions were intact, and their powder was dry. Foote was also able to locate and pull ashore the carronade they had brought with them, along with some ball and chainshot. Foote sent Emmanuel Clevis and a Muskogee named Josephus to Key west in the dinghy, armed to the teeth, to steal them another boat. Meanwhile he and his men waited, fished, and watched the threatening skies. Clevis and Josephus returned five days later with the stolen sloop *Earnestine*, two kegs of Burgundy, and the news of Bowles' death.

Foote fumed for three days, while his men feasted on Conch and mussels and the weather gradually abated. Then the small trade ship *Santa Sophia* had the extreme bad fortune to come over the horizon. Foote, mobilized his men and mounted the carronade on the bow of the *Earnestine*. Although heavily outgunned by even the tiny trade boat, he utilized a trick used by Bowles in similar circumstance, disguising the gun with tarps until his vessel, with the crew smiling and waving, was point blank to the Spanish ship's hull. The *Santa Sophia* was sitting on the bottom in forty feet of water within the hour, her crew butchered, the beneficiaries of Foote's rage at the Spanish.

It was then that the crew noticed the masts of three other wrecks driven on the reefs by the last several days of storms.

This began a relatively lucrative career of wrecking, already an honored tradition in Key West, on the part of the inhabitants of Perrin's Island, punctuated by brief sessions of malicious piracy directed at the Spanish trade. In short order, a series of stilt shanties grew up on the island, and the men used their newfound wealth to bring back household necessities, rum, and of course, women. Foote himself took as mate(without, it should be noted, benefit of clergy) Columbine Switt, a flower of Virginia who had run away with her merchantman lover only to have been unceremoniously dumped in St. Croix. Perrin's Island was well on it's way to becoming a community.

3: Tuesday

Kate walked to school Tuesday like always. Everything had to be like always. She would walk down Tarpon street and then along the docks to the bridge, and every morning there would sit *Ganymeade*, the Weekender she had built lovingly with her dad. The Weekenders were a classic design, archaic in some ways, and beautiful, and her dad had lavished care on every inch of it. The boat could have been built simply, but Ganymeade was all polished wood, with flourishes in the knees he had carved himself and a masthead that she had only just come to realize was probably his mother's face. Her face as well.

Like always, she ran her hand along the rubrail as she passed, feeling her father's presence.

Her mom had remarried--far too soon for her tastes--at the urging of their minister to a man he had hand-picked, someone being groomed for power. Paul, her step father, was not a brute. He simply wasn't very interesting or very interested. He was a man on his way up, a man who wanted the symbology and respectable cache of a family. Getting no younger, with a failed marriage behind him and no time to waste, he had now acquired a wife, a daughter, a house, and could move on to more important things; business things, and politics. Paul had wasted no time "cleaning house," rapidly selling off all those things of his predecessor that he could liquidate without major strife. Some things Kate threw a fit about, mostly memorabilia, and mostly she got her way. Kate's mom mostly stayed out of it. Some things apparently disappeared into "that rat hole" of an attic, things Kate's mom remembered being around, that simply never rematerialized. "Robert got a little erratic there at the end" she would sigh, "who knows where they went?"

Kate did.

It was only the boat that had caused Paul real problems. Despite his intention to sell it "to help pay for college" (yeah, right), the boat had been left in Robert's will specifically to Kate, to be held in trust for her until her 18th birthday. Kate refused to budge, and with no clear title, there were no buyers. "Fine" Paul had said finally "let it rot there, but you're paying the dockage fees." Kate said she would. Paul had pulled everything out of the boat that looked salable and had recoded the lock to keep her out of it.

But hinges can be removed, locks can be recoded. . . . .

As for the things that had vanished, they had mysteriously found their way into the space behind a loose piece of baseboard in her bedroom, and from there into the **Ganymeade**.

Kate crossed the bridge and walked to her school, a crumbling 50's brick building oddly out of place in

Florida. She felt strangely, blissfully calm, as if the whole adventure was already over. Getting in was the usual, searching the bags, and the frisk, and the metal detector, and swiping her ID. Had things always been this controlled? She didn't remember. At homeroom, she got an rfid tag so she could go with impunity through the halls to the main office with her paperwork, paperwork that explained in the most arcane legalese that it was more than all right if she was late to school tomorrow, that her dentist required her attention. The secretary glanced at the papers.

"You have the same dentist as Sandra Walker? She was just in here."

She tried to look blasé'. "Dunno, maybe. He's going on vacation."

Kate had no idea at all what she meant by that, but it seemed to satisfy the woman. She watched as her paperwork was dropped into a chipped plastic 'to be filed' bin. The game, her father had said, was not fucking up, not being sued, not being noticed. As long as there was a paper trail and their butts were covered, he said, they never asked what was really going on.

She was home free.

The rest of the day sort of swam by. It was unusually hot for early spring, and the air conditioning wasn't on yet. The windows were open and a humid breeze full of magnolia and loam was meandering into the classrooms. Everyone seemed drowsy, even the teachers. She would have been, were it not for the electric arc of anticipation running up her spine. Part of her was asleep, and part of her was burning.

At chapel, she didn't dare sit with Sandy, didn't dare look her direction. But the pillars of the meeting hall were covered with gold filigreed mirrors in a style her father had called "trailer park rococo" and she chanced a glance off the glass. Sandy was looking at her, watching her in the reflection. She looked away immediately, but her eyes had been bright. Burning.

Her homework had gotten done like usual in the afternoon. Dinner was as cool and uneventful as ever, and the hours between dinner and bedtime, staring with the family at sanitized "family" television, were interminable.

That evening, she only listened to her radio for an instant, just enough to assure herself that the signal had been real, then back into hiding it went. She didn't call Sandy. Nothing, nothing must give them away.

Sandy.

They had grown up together, played together as kids, laughed together in the days before Kate's father died and their world had turned so dark and adult. They had acted out domestic scenes--some of them oddly sexual--with dolls and braided one another's hair and went happily sailing with Kate's dad and talked endlessly of boys and boys and summer and boys.

But Kate's dad had died, and the boys had turned out to be hopelessly young and clumsy, and their lives began becoming more and more chaperoned and limited as they moved past being children. Sandy had had her first kiss in the back of the bus to band camp from a boy named

Clint who had then humiliated her by telling everyone about it. Kate's had been from a neighbor boy on her back porch, about a month before his folks divorced and he'd moved away. Sandy was the pretty one, stylish, with exotic looks, who was invited to dance after dance after dance and had gotten herself a black eye for saying 'no' to a member of the football team and had walked home angry and in tears and very much virgo intacta. Kate had attracted the outcasts and had lost her virginity in the back of a car to a boy she barely knew 'just to get rid of the damn thing.' Neither Sandy's reticence nor Kate's willingness had bought either of them a ticket to the 'happy ever after' they were always being promised in the Morals and Futures classes they were required to take.

So they dated the stupid boys, and spent hours and hours on their cell phones with one another, talking late, late into the night. They went to the beach together and splashed in the water and talked endlessly of boys and kisses and sex and blowjobs and a billion small and horribly important things.

So in a way, it wasn't surprising that when Sandy's folks were out of town and she was sleeping over at Kate's that they should talk of kissing. And it wasn't surprising when, after failing to find the words to describe the kiss this dork boy from the ministerial alliance had tried to lay on her, that Sandy would turn to demonstration, which, of course led Kate to a story and demo of her own. Then they fell to a discussion and scientific exploration of the *perfect* kiss, what it would be composed of and how it would feel and how it would be delivered. . .

. . .which of course led to something else entirely.

They were young, but they weren't stupid. They knew what had happened. They knew that their long friendship and affection had finally, inevitably turned to romance and passion. They knew, crushingly, that the fairy tale romantics they had sought from the boys they had suddenly stumbled across in each other.

Kate had puzzled all through the schoolday how to discuss this, how to talk to Sandy about what had happened. She fretted over whether this had been the same for Sandy or if it was all just some game she was playing in her head. She panicked over making a fool of herself in front of her very best friend in the whole world, and of poisoning that most crucial of her relationships by being stupid. But in the end, there had been no worry. Sandy had simply bounded up to her after chapel, all flushed and out of breath, and said: "I love you. There's not much we can do about that, is there?"

Kate allowed as how there wasn't.

They were young, but they weren't stupid. They also knew that any whisper of this, the slightest breath, would land them in some morals camp being force fed ipecac while they watched pictures of naked women, an 'aversion therapy' designed to make them hate women's bodies and, not coincidentally, their own. That was NOT going to happen.

So they kept dating the stupid boys--and some of the nice ones--who got precious little off of them. They stole kisses in closets and behind the bushes and engineered camping trips together that resulted in sexual explosions between the two of them that approached Sadism and left them exhausted and sweaty and chafed and alive. Otherwise, they were the very souls of discretion, and no one knew. No one at all.

But when Kate's home had become cool and foreign and Sandy's parents began to seriously discuss 'finding their daughter a suitable husband' they knew plans had better be made.

They thought at once of Europe. Who wouldn't? After centuries of war, Europe had become the light of the world. Overly bureaucratic, perhaps, but a place of peace and relative liberty, regularly excoriated in the Federal press for "failure to take into account American interests." They thought of ways to get to the now closeted paradise of Iceland, ways to cross the fortified border with Canada, ways to reach the new, shining cities of Surinam and Venezuela. All of them so far out of reach. All of them requiring money and contacts and information they had no way to obtain.

But there sat Ganymeade. Bottom still clean, sails still intact, every line and tackle lovingly cared for by Kate. And thinking of the Ganymeade brought back her father's stories of the fleet and of sailing the Cay Sal before most of it submerged under the rising seas. In the fleet, if they took you, you took a crew name and identity. From that point on, you were whomever you wanted to be. The Fleet saw no race, no religion, no gender. They had cordial relationships with the Caribbean islands, with Venezuela, even, it was rumored with Brussels and Reykjavik.

It became an option, or, rather, it was their only option.

Sandy. Kate thought of her eyes, her wide mouth and crooked smile, the coolness of her skin and the way her soft face felt in the darkness. She curled in on herself, sliding her hand between her legs, and let Sandy and the darkness take her away, while out on the darkened sea, hope was speaking to the universe at 75 watts.

4:   The Foote Princes

Pressed by the colonial governments of surrounding islands on the question of national allegiance, the islanders found themselves in a bit of a quandary. They hated the Spanish and Americans, they felt betrayed by Britain's acquiescence to Bowle's capture and subsequent demise, and, well, none of them spoke French. Even the Muskogee and Creek had rejected them, which left the settlers with the fragments of Bowles' ambitious dreams and the danger of being overrun as a colonial tidbit for the taking. There was no choice in the matter. They declared themselves a nation.

Jonathan Foote's men has always addressed him by the honorific of "Chief", for such was Bowles' title among the Muskogee (technically Bowles had been War Chief of the Muskogee and simultaneously a Colonel in the British Army), a practice which remained until his death. Knowing the European fascination with their own monarchs, though, the islanders referred to him to the outside world as "King." This was later changed to "Prince" as being more in keeping with a monarch whose domain included only seven acres of land and about forty subjects. So it came to pass that Jonathan Foote became Prince Jonathan I, Warchief of the Perrin Muskogee, Thunder of the Seas, Protector of the realm and all its Environs, and Lord of the New Muskogee Empire. Few were impressed.

Impressed or not, the island prospered, plundering wrecks on the reefs, acting as a stopping point for fishing vessels, and assisting the odd smuggling operation. By the 1840's, there were about a hundred Muscogans, living on stilt houses or on vessels moored in the island's lee. Wealth not usable on the island was stashed in banks in a half-dozen locations, enough so that when the island was razed by a hurricane in the fall of 1847, Jonathan and the surviving founding fathers were able to rebuild with new, not wrecked, timber, supplied from the growing lumber mills in, of all places, Pensacola.

The life was surprisingly good, surprisingly easy. The island was perfectly placed to transfer goods from small trade ships of one flag to another, a great place to bypass customs fees and shipping taxes. With the nominal control of Jonathan I's monarchy, the place was safer than most port towns, the whisky better, the women for hire cleaner, prettier, and more reliable.

For his part, Jonathan was happy. He was respected, and though not filthy rich, he had everything he had ever wanted. His men credited him with their success. His woman adored him.

Adored? Columbine worshipped Jonathan as he had worshipped William Bowles. Abandoned by her lover and rejected by her family, she had seen no possible end for herself but whoring, sickness, and death. Jonathan had swept her away from all that, had made her a queen. Again and again, in gratitude, love, and desire she had tried to give him an heir, only to fail to catch again and again. She attributed it to her frail disposition, to the dissolute life she'd led before him. In fact it was probably just the first instance of the generally low rate of fertility that would plague the Foote princes for all of their reign. Finally, one night when the stifling hot skies were traced with lightning and the sea was roaring, Columbine came to her Prince, and knew that he had filled her with a child.

Columbine bore Jonathan a single son. The boy, named Purdee William Foote, grew to strapping manhood, was educated in Bermuda and England, and, when Jonathan Foote grew ill in 1853 of a progressive skin cancer, took the reins of power. Purdee Foote, with the smiling acquiescence of his parents, became Prince Jonathan II, Lord of Perrin Island. Confident, handsome, and with contacts in Europe and the Caribbean, Purdee seemed an heir assured of success.

It was under Purdee's reign that the island enjoyed its greatest prosperity. He engaged in a vigorous campaign to increase the island's size, based on careful observation of the erosion and sand accretion of the tidal areas. Through careful placement of posts and waddling, Purdee and the second generation of islanders managed to increase Perrin island to nearly 14 acres, the bulk of it at least four feet above mene high tide. He used his multiple contacts in England and in the Southern United States to great advantage, issuing impromptu flags of convenience to slavers and providing passports and letters of introduction to nearly anyone who cared to apply. . . . .for a fee, of course. . . .The coffer's swelled. By this time, the nation had over 20 large buildings ashore--albeit on stilts-- as well as a navy that boasted two armed sloops and three gun galleys. The best days were yet to come.

5:   Libertad

Kate woke before her alarm, surprisingly refreshed, surprisingly ready. She showered and brushed her teeth and dressed. She looked at herself in the mirror, cargo pants and a T-shirt, an outfit she'd worn last week on this same day. Nothing curious there.

She zipped open her bag and extracted "Our Homeland," the massive history text they practically had to memorize, along with her copy of Rev. Jeeder's "Religious Fallacies and how to Combat them." from her Morals and Futures class. She hid them between two blankets in her closet. Out from behind the baseboard came the last of her treasures. In the place of the texts in her book bag went the radio, some clothes, and a wooden box with some memories and a handful of .38 special rounds. Then her math book went back on top, just in case anyone looked. From a dirty, strangely heavy sock behind the wall, she took her dad's old Smith and Wesson Combat Masterpiece, a revolver that had been his father's and that her mom knew zero about ("tell her and she'll throw it out" he'd said). He'd taught her ages ago how to work it, taught her until she was a better shot than he is, killing cans out at sea. Now she loaded the pistol, leaving an empty chamber under the hammer, just in case, and slid it into one of the side zipper pockets of her book bag, just in case.

One last look around. Replace the baseboard. Make the bed. Deep breath.

Downstairs, Paul commented that she was up early. He never looked up from his Very Important Email.

"I need to catch Sandy before class and give her a handout she's missing. Oh, hey, I could be a couple of minutes late getting home. Gloria and Stephen are meeting me after chapel to go over our history notes. We want to make sure we all have everything."

Her mother started to say something, but Paul, still at his computer, chimed in with "good idea" and that was that.

She thought of kissing her mom goodbye, but then she never did, and as much as it felt right, it would've made the day different. So she just said goodbye and that she'd call if she'd run late and snagged an apple and headed out the door.

It wasn't until after she heard the screen close behind her and she rounded the corner that she could stop clamping down on her breathing. She took another deep breath and moved on. Normal, normal, normal....down Tarpon, as usual, then right along the docks toward the bridge, and there was **Ganymeade**, as usual, and she runs her hand along the rubrail, as usual, only this time, with a quick glance around, she swings aboard.

Snap, snap, and the sailcover is off and on the floor of

the cockpit and she's pulling on the mainsheet halyard and the gaff is set. She slips the bow line, and the stern, and hauls in the sheet and the boat is away, picking up speed. The wind is freshening, and from onshore, which is perfect, and the Ganymeade slides through the water and into the channel. And two miles down the shore she can see, on the crumbling dock out back of the Walmart parking lot, a single figure in black.

Sandy.

Kate luffs the sail, the boat slows and glides by, and Sandy just steps aboard. The sheet goes tight, and they're off for the channel again. Neither of them speak. Sandy's eyes are luminous, her breath short, her body coiled like she's ready to jump into the water if anything happens. No words. When they round #18 and head for the cut, Sandy suddenly gets this startled look and says "PHONES!"

They dig for their cell phones, clink them like wine glasses, and hurl them into the water. For nearly two years the phones were their lifeline. Now the gps chips would betray their position. No one to talk to anyway.

It isn't until the great red square of #1 slides past the port side and they enter open ocean that Sandy relaxes. She slides over to Kate, plants a warm, wet kiss on her neck, and wraps herself around her, holding tight. Kate closes her eyes. For a moment, just a moment, they're home.

6:   Lacy

Columbine, consort to the Prince of Perrine Island, died of influenza in the spring of 1853, a slow and lingering death. The elder Jonathan, ever the devoted mate, was inconsolable. "When we put her in the sea," Purdee wrote to schoolmate Leonard Scott, "she took his heart with her." Prince Jonathan I, father of his nation, followed his bride into the depths two months later.

In March of 1857, Leonard Scott visited Perrin's Island en route to New Orleans. He was later to write to his aunt in London:

"I found Purdee a man transformed. At school he had seemed a ruffian, though a nice enough fellow in his way. I now found him regal and commanding, and the respect his men, even his father's old henchmen, pay him is inspiring. One would rather think him the son of royalty rather than the offspring of pirates".

Scott returned to London full of stories about the Island and its wild and noble inhabitants. The Prince's Renaissance was yet to come. The American Civil War was coming, and with it, a Golden Age for the Muscogee Empire. Like most of the British, and with a Floridian legacy, Purdee was firmly on the side of the Confederacy, and for the entire length of the war, did a quiet and effective trade with Confederate blockade runners and raiders in powder, shot, coal, and foodstuffs. He would calmly send his own ships under Muscogee or French flags up the US coast to Boston harbor, pick up a load of materials, and then sell them to support Confederate naval activities....at a profit, of course. His customers included not only runner vessels, but such illustrious confederate raiders as the *Alabama* and the sidewheeler *Florida*. A single federal expedition was mounted against the island from Ft. Jefferson in the dry Tortugas, but the flotilla, consisting of an unnamed frigate (Probably the aging *Samuel Hayes*) and four armed sloops never returned. Since no incident is recorded in the annals of the island, it must be inferred that the vessels perished, not by shot, but in the unpredictable weather around the Florida straits.

The defeat of the Confederacy was a financial victory for the island, despite the Prince's disappointment. War itself had been vastly profitable, despite the charity Purdee had personally shown to the Confederacy, and had concluded with the influx of a great deal of Southern hard coin moving out of the way of the advancing Union forces. Bluntly, the islanders were rich. The island expanded, stabilized by new construction and planting, to nearly 20 acres. Purdee himself lived like some oriental potentate, in a stilt house with nine rooms and four young women. The Muscogan fleet now included two former Confederate privateers, the armed sloop *Edna Jean*, and the steam screw schooner *Tallahassee,* a formidable vessel mounting eight brass

6-pounders Life was good to the Muscogan Imperials, and the only blight on the reign of Johnathan II was his apparent inability--though certainly not for want of trying--to produce an heir.

At about the turn of the 20th century, the island's population stood officially at 560. If this seems excessive, it should be noted that his highness had for some years been in the practice of selling citizenships (and new identities) to anyone with the appropriate cash. The actual resident population is estimated to have been around 130, most living in boats moored in the lee of the island. Purdee issued the island's first currency. . . .actually two currencies: The Royal Pound, referred to locally as "script" and supposedly representing a percentage of royal holdings, it was used for trade with neighboring islands, particularly the Bahamas, Cayman Brac, and Cay Sal, which was then a going concern. Purdee also minted in Brazil a hard coin, struck in .999 silver, with his likeness and the island's flag. This silver nestegg more than once was to bail the Empire out of hard times.

For now, though, business was good and getting better, with the upcoming Spanish-American conflict anticipated as a twofold delight. First, for the income it would produce e, and second, as a payback to the Cuban Spanish for the death of William Bowles.

Unfortunately, fate intervened.

In September of 1897, with the islanders gearing up for the income that the announcement of the the Cuban revolution by Marti two years earlier was bound to bring, a storm hit the island. It skirted the Bahamas with 60 mile an hour winds and then came suddenly west, gaining power as it did. By the time it struck Perrine island, the winds were in excess of 100 miles an hour, pushing ahead of it a nine-foot storm tide. Purdee, no stranger to the Gulf, wisely ordered his people into their boats and their anchor lines played out to their fullest extent. His foresight was probably responsible for saving at least a hundred lives.

The Storm was hellish. Through the rain and spray the horrified islanders could see the mammoth waves smashing into the frail stilt houses on the submerged island. Anchor lines snapped like string, sending small ships careening northwest with the wind. Purdee, aboard *Tallahassee*, spent a full eleven hours at the helm fighting to keep the storm reefed ship and its balky auxiliary into the wind. Finally, her storm anchor gave way, and the schooner reeled northwest. After a godawful night, the wind abated, and Purdee was able to limp his damaged ship back home.

The sight that met them some five hours later was disheartening. Not a single structure remained standing on the island, which was still fully submerged under the storm tide and visible only as a tangle of uprooted mangrove and wreckage standing in the water. Some of the smaller boats had swamped in the storm, and their masts protruded wanly from the turbulent waters. Amazingly, no loss of life at all was reported.

Johnathan II set in immediately to rebuild, but many of the islanders had had the heart knocked out of them. About half the population took what they could salvage (along with their sizable foreign bank holdings) and removed themselves to the British Virgin Islands, or to the Keys, content to live off their savings. Undaunted,

Purdee and a few followers cleared the rubble, and, when the waters sub sided, began to remake the island.

Without the impetus of War, however, and with the flight of so much manpower and capital, the job was slow and arduous. The much anticipated war between the Americans and Spain came and went in what seemed like moments, and an American occupation for the "security" of Cuba ended the Marti revolution almost before it started. By 1910, the island was only back to its original 7 acres and there were only six standing structures. Purdee, by now an old man, was dispirited. The once-lucrative Empire he had built from his father's island was now barely able to support its residents, and worse times were yet to come. Attempting to capitalize on the Great War, the Muscogans found themselves suddenly and unceremoniously snatched up by the British Navy, divided, and dumped in various locations from Key West to the Bahamas. The Muscogans had, it seemed, developed an unfortunate tendency to sell fuel to the Kaiser's submarines, and enough was enough.

Purdee Foote, the Prince of Muscogee, found himself in a small house on Key Largo under nominal guard. Old and ill, he resigned himself to his fate and was in the process of writing his memoirs and awaiting his inevitable end when a remarkable thing happened.

That remarkable thing was Jacklyn Lacy Ferrin, whose family had come to the keys from Atlanta. Jacklyn, a delicate child of 17, was suffering from a chronic inflammation of the pleura which refused treatment. Her father, a methodist minister, had been advised that the girl would not weather another winter in her present condition, and so he had taken the family as far south as he could. Jacklyn and her mother had met Purdee on one of their frequent shell-collecting walks, and the girl became fascinated with the Prince's stories. Every evening she would walk down to Purdee's little cabin, help him cook his dinner, and then kneel adoringly at his feet as he told her his tales. Jacklyn, however, was not just a young girl interested in romantic stories. She developed another agenda.

Perhaps she saw in the old pirate a way out of the stultifying life her father had planned for her. Perhaps she truly developed feelings for the old man......perhaps puberty hit her harder than most...

Whatever, after only about a month of visiting to hear his stories, she turned up pregnant.

Her reverend father was understandably outraged. He descended on Purdee's meager cabin and threatened him with a silver handled cane the Wesley foundation had given him. Purdee ended the argument by blowing the head off the cane with a new broom-handled Mauser he kept for just such an occasion. The Reverend Ferrin left his Highness presence in a hurry and returned with his rebellious daughter in disgrace to Atlanta, where Jacklyn defiantly named her out-of-wedlock child Purdee. There might have ended the story were it not for the foresight of Purdee Sr.

After the Ferrin's departure, Edgar Dees, one of the Prince's last loyal minions, received a letter marked with the seal of his Highness. Dees, in nominal British house arrest in the Bahamas, had thought he'd heard the last of the old man. The letter, some nine pages in all, read in part:

"Edgar, my friend, praise all the gods that tend to pirates, I have an heir. After all these years, the throne finally has a new seat to replace my old behind. . . ."

The letter continued with a series of instructions, exhortations, and more important, account numbers instructing Dees to go secure the new heir and to rebuild the nation. Dees could easily have ignored the letter, pocketed the accounts, and lived in comfort till the end of his days, but the persuasiveness and loyalty commanded by his Highness were not to be denied. Dees corresponded secretly with Jacklyn through her cousin in Jacksonville, and, at the conclusion of the war, smuggled her and young Purdee from under the eagle eye of the Reverend Ferrin and down to the Keys. Johnathan II, alas, was never to see his son. He died, alone but content, in the last month of WWI. His body was buried by followers at sea in 1918 just off Long Key.

Jacklyn may have been a bookish, sickly adolescent, as the cadaverously white skin under her shock of red hair may have testified, but where the legacy of her son was involved, Dees found her a tigress, indomitable to the point of exhaustion. Her cousin, Sarah Jane Cooper of Miami, wrote in 1920:

"She believed all of it, the whole tale the old man had spun for her, and I must admit, the first time I saw her there, this little girl surrounded by pirates and smugglers and all of them fawning and kneeling to her in earnest, I began to believe it myself. . . . "

7: The Admiralty

The fleet was nervous. The tropical storm had forced them too far north into the Gulf, and now their return path was taking them way too close to the Americans. American jets had been overflying them at ridiculously low altitudes, trying to prompt a response. American rpv's played chicken with fleet rpv's, each looking for information and opportunity. Fleet ships released balloons, forcing the jets higher.

The Admiral was on ansible link, his small boat *Dragonfly* pressing on in the midst of the chaos of the fleet, mercifully anonymous beneath the gaze of the American's targeting systems.

"what do we got?"

Casey, his master at arms, hovered in a slightly strobing image in the ansible plate. Rosalie, the Bosun, was listening, but incoming text only, beneath the fleet in a submersible. It was so much easier when they were rafted.

"The barrage balloons have pushed them up above 5000

feet. We got some contacts with the navy out of Pensacola, and they're really happy we did that. It was the morons in DC that had them buzzing us. The navy doesn't need any more problems. Oh, somebody named Silverman sends his regards, Admiral."

The Admiral smiled. Jas Silverman was commandant of Pensacola NAS. He was also an old friend.

"Casey, have we completed the turn?"

Casey Grimaced. "Most of us. Some of the small lug riggers couldn't point high enough and have swung a bit far east, but they're correcting and catching up."

"How far?"

"The outer fringe is only about 22 miles out of U.S. Territorial. Too fucking close."

<<Rosie>>[[Can we herd them in?]]

"We can try."

"Casey, get your outrunners out to the rim and get us tightened up. Tow some of the stragglers if you have to. Rosie, as soon as we clear Ft. Jefferson, we'll cut back southeast and make a hard cross. Wind should be with the stream by then so we should have fairly smooth water. We'll raft at the mouth of the Nicholas."

<<Rosie>>[[On it.]]

"I'll be over on the *Asklepius* if you need me"

"Admiral, I don't need to tell you...."

"No, you don't. I'm switching boats with Rodney, and I'll dock with his O'day"

"Just so you're careful. We know they're watching."

<<Rosie>>[[he knows]]

Marcus cut the link. It had been fifteen years or so since he'd become Marcus and become Admiral, and this was the best crew he'd ever had, and they'd better be. The fleet was swelling with refugees, and the Americans seemed to be more insane than usual.

He unlashed the tiller and waved to Rodney, and the two boats began edging together. Rodney was a good kid. He and old Lucius traded off running one of the fleet's FM stations. They had done this a dozen times, playing a boat to boat shell game to make sure the Admiral's whereabouts remained, at the very least, confusing. As the boom from Rodney's O'day crossed over his cockpit, they switched vessels. Marcus swung the little O'day to the east, headed for Asklepius.

Asklepius was a hospice boat, and Iron Bess, the Admiral's companion for thirty years, was dying.

Whataya gonna do?

8:   On the Water

It was after noon now, and the fear was that they would
come in behind the fleet, and that with the
Ganymeade's slow hull speed, they'd never catch up
and be out on the open water with, literally, no where to
go. But the signal from the fleet grew steadily, and
using the little radio as a direction finder as her father
had shown her, the fleet was north of them, and
approaching. With any luck they'd be swept up in the
middle of it without any worries.

Kate had really wondered. She had wondered if they
could pull this off. She had wondered if they should.
She had wondered if they would get to sea and regret it,
lose the force and passion that had driven them out
here.

But Sandy's face was still bright. She made them
sandwiches--ridiculously big, ponderous things--and
extracted kisses as payment. The land had been hot,
but the water was cool and Sandy curled around her,
danced around the tiny boat, laughed and giggled and
cried with joy. She was a wonder, a genii's bottle that
was finally coming uncorked. Kate couldn't take her

eyes off of Sandy.

At 3:00 PM they knew the dice had been rolled. School would be out, and if no one had reported their failure to return after their "appointments" then their failure to make it home would soon be noted. Kate's mom would be first. She would probably fret for an hour, then try Kate's now-submerged cell phone, then call the school, then Sandy's mom. Then the whole messy process of finding them would swing into action. They had left preciously few clues. Sooner or later someone would notice that *Ganymeade* was awol, and might put two and two together, but hopefully, that would take some time. Time, at 4 1/2 knots, was what they desperately needed.

About 4:30, they saw the first boat, a tiny lateen rigged Tortuga, moving parallel to them. Just the sort of boat that would be in the fleet. They didn't see the sharpie until it was almost on them. Moving under electric and sail, the long, narrow boat swung in behind them, two 20mm muzzles at the bow tracking them careful. This was a militia ship, and as scary as it was, it meant they were within the fleet.

The fleet patrol boat edged up beside them, a mottled hull blending with the water, virtually invisible clear crabclaw sails, and a crew in full body armor. Kate had studied. She knew this boat, every inch of it. She knew it was a Vesper class patrol boat, a 37 foot glass and ply sharpie bristling with weapons. She knew how fast its biodiesel-electrics could drive it, how large the crew compliment. She knew its range. What she didn't know was how this was going to go, how they would be received.

The patrolboat leveled it's sails and matched speed with its electrics, gliding silently only about a foot off the *Ganymeade's* starboard side. The skipper was a man in his late 60's from the look of him, with a wild mane of white hair and a full beard draped artfully over his chest armor. He looked them up and down and simply said: "Good afternoon, ladies."

"Afternoon skipper." Kate noted that the crew of the patrol was not relaxed. Apparently two girls on a little sailboat were to be treated as a threat until proven otherwise.

"You're quite a ways from the mainland. Do you need navigational assistance to get back home?"

Kate had practiced this line for nearly a year: "No sir, we here here by intent. We intend to join the crew of the fleet." She felt Sandy's arm slide around her, warm.

The skipper smiled. He glanced down, noting that the *Ganymeade* already had her bumpers out.

"Heave to and prepare to be boarded."

Kate had barely time to luff her sail before her little boat was made fast to the patrol ship and was literally swarming with fleet militia. The inspection was surprisingly quick and surprisingly thorough. Everything, even the water tank, was probed. Kate had a small, anxious moment when they found her father's pistol, but the militawoman that found it merely glanced at the gun with a professional interest and returned it to it's place.

And then they were gone, leaving only their skipper.

"You see that tortuga there at about 11:00 o'clock?

Kate nodded.

"You've got about the same hullspeed. Follow it. We'll be sailing for about three days, maybe four, before we raft. When we raft, raft next to her. Got it?" He glanced at *Ganymeade's* stern. "You've already got rafting planks. You *have* been planning this a while, haven't you lass?"

Kate grinned.

"Stay with the tortuga. Goin' off on your own right now would be a bad idea, you understand? You've a CB in there. We monitor 6. If you get lost or get in trouble, give a shout out to Navigation, and they'll direct you. Making any other transmissions would also be a bad idea. Got it?

They nodded in unison.

The old skipper effortlessly swung back onto his own vessel. He did it without thought, a man utterly in tune with living on the sea.

"good luck...." he said, and after a moment"....and welcome."

The patrol ship raised her crabclaw sails up from horizontal and swung across the stern of the little Weekender, gaining speed. Kate pulled in her sheet and headed for the tortuga, now bobbing in the distance. it took her a moment to realized how fast she was breathing. She and Sandy just looked at each other for a long time, slowing themselves down.

Then they laughed and shouted until they were horse.

9.   The Foote Princes

Jacklyn became the undisputed driving force of the
island. The Islanders, many of them pirates and
smugglers by nature, learned to respect her judgement
(and her accuracy with the broomhandle Mauser left her
by Jonathan II). By Purdee Jr.s ninth birthday, Jacklyn
had reestablished the colony on Perrin with a population
of 55 and was reaping a lively living assisting smugglers
who were transporting rum from Cuba into the now-dry
America. Purdee Jr. was schooled in the Bahamas, with
frequent trips home. By 1938, when Purdee returned
to the island for good, the business had changed.
Jacklyn, still running on the ragged edge of her delicate
health, was using her heavily fortified island to assist
refugees. The unfortunates, most of them Jewish,
homosexual, or Communist, had gotten to Cuba by way
of Spain only to be detained by Cuban authorities or
American immigration. At considerable risk, Jacklyn's
ships slipped into the marshes near Mariel to bring them
to Perrin, and from there to the Virgins or to the
clutter of inlets and bayous that is the Northern Gulf.
Purdee II felt good about the work that they were doing.
Apparently the families of those brought in felt so too.
Their rewards to the crown were generous. As for the

Cubans, the traditional enemies of the Muscogans, during their lone gunboat sortie against the island they learned a fundamental lesson of military physics: Small islands make better gun platforms than small gunboats do.

On Nov. 29, 1940, just nine days before the Japanese attack on Pearl Harbor, the health of the Iron Queen of Perrin Island finally failed her. A fortnight before, an unexpected cold wave had come in from the Northwest, sweeping the island with a wet, chilly wind. Purdee Jr. later wrote :

"Mother never could take the cold. In fact, if she could've, she never would've met my father. She would go about wrapped in a down vest and poncho at the slightest drop in temperature. The winter that year, as I remember, began early and was particularly nasty. Mother sat most of the day on the veranda that ran round her house, wrapped in blankets and sipping hot tea and yellng at the clouds for them to leave the sun alone. I finally told her to go in. [over the next few days] she declined rapidly. She took hot bath after hot bath, and kept herself swaddled in blankets, but she still complained of being chilled. Her skin seemed to hang away from her and took on an odd transparency. I'll always remember that. We--both of us--knew she was dying. Still, she played the grand dame to the end. . . "

On the evening of November 29th, with a gale wind shuddering the house, Jacklyn called Purdee, his lieutenant Jack Marks, and a vacationing American flyer and a buddy of Marks' named William Cunningham, into her presence. There, with those witnesses, she formally tranferred power to her son. Purdee became Prince Jonathan III, Lord of the Perrin Muscogee. He kissed her on the forehead and she asked for some hot cider. By the time it arrived from the kitchen, she was gone.

Jacklyn Lacy Ferrin, who called herself Jacklyn Ferrin Foote, was buried at sea on December 1, 1940, with over 60 vessels in attendance. She was posthumously named Queen Jacklyn, and so took her place in the line of succession of the Chieftains of the Perrin Muscogee. Six days later, the whole world was at war.

World War II was a difficult time for the Empire, and especially for Jonathan III. Ill-accustomed to command, he had a difficult time holding his mother's coalition together. He lacked his parent's charisma, and it was only through his own stoicism in the face of personal and national tragedies that finally won him the respect of his own men.

In defense of Purdee Jr., there was little he could have done. The Gulf and Caribe states swarmed with espionage and the waters swarmed with Nazi submarines. Suspicion was everywhere, especially of the Islanders. Purdee offered his vessels first to the U.S., then to the British, but there were no takers. His ships were invariably searched on entering port and invariably detained on leaving. No one knew quite what to make of the Perrin islanders. Certainly, no one trusted them. Purdee, for his part, was determined to make at least SOME contribution to the destruction of the Axis. He continued running refugees to safe ports, turning his ships now to Nicaragua instead of the heavily patrolled Florida coast and entering into an often bizarre ad-hoc intelligence operation with American expatriates in Cuba, including, oddly, the author Earnest

Hemingway, who made one unannounced appearance on the island and was treated as a kind of visiting dignitary (which seemed to have rather unnerved him). Purdee used his piratical loyalists to "lean" on Nazi sympathizers in Grand Cayman and the Caribbean and provided intelligence tidbits to the British wherever possible.

Nonetheless, it was a hard time. Purdee took a mate, in the family tradition, named Margaret Spencer, who had been living in Freeport in the Bahamas. A scant five months later, her skiff capsized en route to the Keys, and she drowned. Purdee swallowed his pain and buried himself in his maritime underground railway.

The end of the war brought a welcome relief to Purdee's kingdom. The conditions in the Gulf islands had been steadily easing through the last year and it looked like trade and prosperity would gradually return to the region. By 1949, the island once again could find fuel to sell to fishermen and smugglers and the trade between the islands in the Gulf and Caribbean was once again flowing unimpeded. It was in 1951 that the first of a series of blows struck.

It was, once again, the weather.

A storm came barreling up the warm water corridor they call "hurricane alley" and smashed the island flat. The houses--all of them--were ripped from their stilts. Breakwaters and docks were pounded to splinters and floated away, and the island remained submerged under a storm tide for nearly two days. Again, as many times in its history, the islanders, led by their Prince, began to rebuild. Five weeks later, with repairs only partially completed, a squall slammed the island, scattering newly laid planks like straw and eroding the island badly.

Purdee was forced to scour the Bahamas and Florida for former Islanders and ask them for assistance. It took a month to raise the money, but this time Purdee was determined to protect the island once and for all. He would spend the money to build a hefty breakwater and docks that would keep the islanders out of the sea. In July, construction on a mammoth dock and breakwater complex began, with wooden cofferdams and molds being filled with island debris and stiffened with iron rebar. Doing the work in summer was a risk, it being hurricane season, but the island was lucky, and work continued through the summer months without a hitch. Still, by the end of October, when the concrete casting began, with the season concluding and work still in progress, many of the islanders breathed a sigh of relief.

Then the storm came.

10:   Paul

It had worked out just as they'd planned: It had been
nearly 5:00 before Kate's mother began to worry. She
had called Kate's cell and left messages--she knew
reception was sketchy at the school. It wasn't until
Sandy's parents had both gotten home from work and
found their daughter gone and called Kate's mom that
panic began to set in. They called the school--which was
closed--they called every one of Katie's friends they
knew of. They drove around the neighborhood.

By this time, Paul was home and grandly took charge.
He called the police and Rev. Winthrop and, without
second thought, the press.

Oddly, the police treated the two girl's disappearance as
two unrelated events. Sandy, ever the devious one, had
seeded the school and her parent's psyche with vague
ideas that there was "some boy" she was interested in,
someone who may or may not have been assigned or
might be assigned or was being assigned as cannon
fodder to the growing counterinsurgent war in Bolivia.
In her room, in a carefully constructed jewel box full of

deceptions, there were military patches and a PX ration book. That, and a couple of condoms. It was all perfect.

Then there was the matter of Sandy's completely undistinguished lower-middle-class working parents, uninteresting people with no noteworthy political or church connections, and really very little else to interest the police or the press. No political advantage there. No ratings. If this working class family's little slutty daughter had run off with some solder, well, so be it.

But Kate was another matter. She had simply and deliberately dropped off the face of the earth, leaving no clues at all for her family. And Paul, the up and coming young politico, could play it to the hilt. Two days after her disappearance, with a weeping wife by his side, he held a press conference emotionally begging the kidnappers to "return his little girl," including a slap at contemporary culture, a plea for more police powers and ending in a prayer session. It was perfect politics, and the state press ate it up. Even two years later, the tabloids were still finding "dramatic revelations" about Kate's kidnapping.

The police wasted no time. "Foreigners" and an "alleged satanist" were rounded up. Press conferences were held. Dramatic clues revealed and then quietly dispensed with when they went nowhere. It was a Circus, a Sideshow. It was a Farce.

Six weeks later, Paul had been walking by the docks when he noticed *Ganymeade* was missing. He had called his insurance company who had, in turn, called the police. No one even made the connection. Good riddance.

For Paul, it was a win-win situation. He got to play the heroic head of a "family too often touched by tragedy." All the press catapulted his position within the party, and he played it to the hilt. Kate's disappearance had the added effect of releasing her college fund, and, along with the insurance money for the boat, he finally had the cash to get the car and the clothes and all the accouterments he would need to move up in the world. His star was on the ascent, and if his bride was drinking herself into an early grave, well, she could be forgiven her grief, being merely a woman, and it was another cross--if an inconvenient one--he could bravely bear before the public.

So clever was Paul that he continued to get milage out of Kate's disappearance for nearly three years, at which point two of his political enemies managed to coax him into the sack with just the wrong teenage intern, but that's another story.

11.   Trials of Empire

It was late in season, and no one expected it. It
flattened Haiti and a day later the port of Guantanemo.
By the time the eye of the storm crossed Perrin Island,
it had sustained winds of 190 knots and was pushing a
58 foot tidal surge ahead of it. Perrin Island, save a
few tenacious mangrove, was gone. Two days later,
Purdee and Jack Marks were surveying the damage,
slogging through mangrove and debris in thigh deep
water. "I wonder" Marks said "what will show at low
tide." "This IS low tide," Purdee had said, "this is all
there is." Marks recalled later that Purdee's face bore
what he had come to call 'the iron look.' It was the look
he had seen when Purdee's wife had died. It was the
look he had seen after the first storm had it. It was the
look that said, I am not going to show you how much this
hurts, and I am not going to stop--ever--until I have
conquered this. At that moment, Marx noted, I finally
accepted him as a Prince.

Over the next four years, Purdee, Jack Marks, and Bill
Cunningham, now a full Naval Commander assigned to air
operations of the Carrier Lexington, scoured the US,
Canada, and the Gulf and Caribbean states for Perrin

Island monies, finding the families of former subjects, finding safety deposit boxes, some of the dating to the turn of the century, full of Johnathan II's hard coin. It was 1959 before the first pile was driven at the island site. Ever so slowly, the island reemerged from the sea. By 1960, the population was 32, and there were nine structures on the island, now a meager five acres of low, dry (mostly) land.

In the early 1960's the situation in the Gulf once again became tight. The Cuban revolutionaries had waltzed themselves calmly into the communist camp (not in any small degree due to the American crushing of Marti's dreams and support for the murderous dictator Batista) and there were rumors of Russian atomic bombs being transported to Cuba. Ships and planes watched the Perrin Island from a hostile distance. Purdee worried, but what was there to be done? Two months before the assassination of the American President John Kennedy, a flight of three jet planes buzzed the island at twilight. No markings were visible. The performance was repeated the next evening, again, just at sundown. The islanders were beginning to talk. Aircraft seldom ventured so close. Things relaxed a bit when the plaines failed to return the following day. Perhaps their curiosity had been satisfied.

But planes returned the next day right at sundown. This time the aircraft type, MIG-15s, was easily identifiable. This time, they strafed.

Explosive rounds ripped through the frail huts on the island and through several of the boats. The planes made two passes. The second time, they were met with a hail of small arms fire, which, although having no visible effect, may have made them less enthusiastic about risking another pass. They departed, leaving in their wake ruined buildings, punctured water tanks, swamped vessels, nine wounded, and four dead. One of the dead was Jack Marks.

Islanders began to drift away. Despite the fact that there was no repeat of the attack, they feared for themselves and their families. By 1965, the island's population was only fifteen, many of them elderly long-term residents. Purdee hoped that the U.S. Vietnam war would spur an increase in population with an influx of draft-dodging young subjects. It didn't happen. By 1970, when the island once again sustained minor damage from a passing storm, the population was only 20. The only influx of population occurred when a dredge and fill operation of island building by a group of Libertarian anarchists in the New Hebrides was abruptly interrupted by Tongan gunboats. The pilgrims, in search of political freedom, sought Perrin Island as an alternative to their failed project, but wanted some constitutional curbs on the Monarchy, and a bill of rights. Like Prince John, Purdee saw the writing on the wall and agreed. Still, the influx barely balanced the attrition of the Island.

In 1968, in a move uncharacteristic for the Foote Princes, Purdee married in a civil ceremony a woman he had met in one of his cash gathering expeditions. Catherine Goldman, herself the granddaughter of an island resident, was the sort of mate he'd always hoped for. She was cultured, calm, strong, and utterly devoted to him. She was also, unfortunately, well past childbearing years, which presented the crown with a problem: what to do for a successor? It was finally agreed that Purdee in his persona of Jonathan III could name a successor, preferably a descendant of one of the original colonists that had accompanied Jonathan Foote to the island in 1820. The trouble was, none could be found. Purdee did what he could: He stalled.

In 1971 his Highness was on a vacation trip with his bride, visiting William Cunningham, now retired, like his Carrier, to Pensacola Florida. At the time, at the behest of Cunningham, he allowed himself to be interviewed by a young reporter from one of the local college newspapers. In the course of three interview sessions, Purdee learned two interesting things. First, he and his young interrogator got along famously. Second, that the young man was himself tied to the island, not by relation to a settler, but by distant blood relation to William Augustus Bowles himself. After a consultation with Cunningham and with two of the island elders, it was agreed that here, at last, was a logical candidate to succeed Purdee on the coral throne. And so it was agreed that, on Purdee's death or abdication, Prince William II, named for Bowles, the Muscogee Warchief, would take the throne. Purdee felt that a huge load had been lifted from him. The torch had been past, and he was finally at peace.

Purdee, Prince Johnathan III, and his wife were killed in a three car collision on the Boca Raton off ramp of the Florida turnpike on Sept. 3, 1975. With them ended the dynasty of the Foote Princes and began a new Reign for the Empire of Muscogee.

Of William II, Bill Cunningham wrote later "there is something about having responsibility, however foreign, thrust on a man that changes him. He either runs from it or the added weight galvanizes him. His Highness is no exception." "All in all, it's an interesting commentary on 'nation' and politics. I mean, look at this situation. Here's this young man, kid really, with a promising future. Suddenly he finds out from interviewing this old goat that, through the most tenuous of connections, he can become heir to a country that, at present, consists mostly of a bunch of old geezers like me and a few yards of mangrove in the Florida Straits. If I hadn't seen the island when it was a going concern, I'd have laughed my ass off. But our present prince took the crown like it was the holy grail or something. He took the island as a sacred trust, passed on to him, and is devoting his whole being to it and his adopted people, however few they are and wherever they may have gotten to. You've got to admire that........I thought the lad was out of his fucking mind."

12:   The Raft

They sailed for four days. While they'd been prepared
for it, taking four hour shifts waking and sleeping was
exhausting, and their fresh water was running out.
They'd managed to catch some water in a rain squall,
and that helped, but if this went on another day or two
they'd be in trouble.

Every day they sailed, the boats got thicker and thicker
as the little tortuga edged closer and closer to the
center of the fleet. Ultimately they had to stay right
off the stern of the tortuga they were following for
fear of losing it. Days were a cluster of sails, some
coming scarily close. Nights they were in a sea of
bobbing lights, trying desperately to make sense of
their position relative to other vessels. Fortunately the
tortuga--named the *Tosca*--had a skipper, a bald
headed man of remarkable physique, who sang opera at
the top of his lungs night and day. It provided an
interesting touchstone for them in the middle of the
crowded night. She had no idea at all how he steered,
sailing solo, and slept.

As nerve-wracking as things could be--and the nights were, at first, a real test--Katie loved it. She loved the fact that they were finally free. She loved being on the ocean. It reminded her of her father, and of a time when she felt she'd really had a family. She loved the fact that she could finally be herself with Sandy. She loved the fact that she could finally be herself with herself.

And Sandy's eccentric passion for her hadn't dimmed in the least. The minute night fell, with Kate on the tiller, Sandy was all over her, hands and warm lips and tongue. It was hard to keep focused on navigation. And then when Sandy took the helm it was Kate's turn. She knew Sandy's body like her own, as Sandy knew hers. She knew that Sandy loved to have her neck kissed. She knew that she loved to have her thighs and stomach gently stroked, and that sucking hard on her pale, compact nipples would bring her to an early, shuddering climax. She always waited till the end of Sandy's watch to jump her so that she could curl up and sleep beside Kate on the warm sea.

Sandy, on the other hand, *never* waited.

Fleet radio was really instructive. Sandy discovered that there were dozens, maybe hundreds, of radio stations in the fleet, some of them probably running little 1/4 watt transmitters that reached only their own cluster of ships. There was every kind of music and programming imaginable, from country to classical to experimental, from spoken word to erotic moans to recorded novels, but it was the voice of the fleet, broadcasting on shortwave, FM and AM, that was *the* source for information. The transmission was relatively powerful, and seemed to skip directions within the fleet, as if several transmitters were handing off the duty throughout the day. The music was solid and eclectic, including live performances from what were apparently fleet musicians. There were talk shows on oceanography and navigation, there was news that would never have been reported on in the states, and every half hour, a weather update and a voice--which Sandy finally decided was synthetic--announcing the center position of the fleet and it's course.

By looking at their charts and comparing the fleet announcements with their gps, the girls figured the fleet to be nearly 20 kilometers across when sailing, proceeding at a stately 4 knots under sail. Katie knew the fleet followed a cycle, from the Gulf of Mexico down--generally through the Nicholas channel--past the Virgin islands and Windwards, and then back into the Caribbean and back to the north, following the winds and currents, avoiding the big storms, sailing when they had to, rafting when they could.

The weather was variable, and one of the days pretty rough. Kate reckoned by their position and the look of the water that that was the Gulf Stream, and counted them lucky to have a West wind. Easterly, against the current, could've meant three metre seas. And after they rounded Cay Sal, and the water had calmed, the command came to raft.

And when the voice of the fleet gave the command to raft, the intrepid crew of the *Ganymeade* realized they hadn't a fucking clue what to do.

Kate pulled alongside to leeward of the *Tosca* and said, somewhat timidly "um, we're supposed to raft with you,

I guess."

And the giant in the little boat just smiled broadly as he dropped his sail. "Yeah, Stephen emailed me. I'd have radioed you, but we try to keep pretty quiet around the Americans, and you seemed to be doing fine." He tossed her a line. "Name's Hank."

"Email?" thought Kate, but what she said was "Stephen?"

"Skipper of the patrol. He asked me to keep an eye out for you."

"Pleased to meet you. I'm Kate, this is Sandy."

Sandy dropped the sail while Kate and Hank lashed their boats together, sterns parallel, and dropped their rafting planks. Their two floating platforms matched each other exactly.

"What are you grinning about?" asked Hank.

"It fits." Kate said happily, "I didn't know until I tried it." Hank just laughed.

The raft came together with astonishing speed. Other boats, unbidden, pulled up beside the *Ganymeade* and *Tosca* and tied on, dropping their own rafting planks. Other vessels rafted opposite them, stern facing stern, and the rafting planks became a 3 metre promenade between lines of boats, no more than 20 in a raft, each raft connected at right angles by a section of floating dock. Within a scant half hour, the hundreds of boats of the fleet had become a large irregular floating island. Adjustments were made, some vessels and raft sections moved here and there, but in less than an hour, raft life had settled in.

Hank, the bald opera buff with the Charles Atlas body, turned out to have been appointed their unofficial guardian (and, in all probability, watchdog). His tiny tortuga, a deckless birdwatcher design no longer than *Ganymeade*, was lined with exercise straps and isometric gizmos, and Hank apparently worked out constantly, even while at the helm.

A man with a pouch and some kind of handheld came down the row of boats, sliding numbered cards into little frames mounted on the sterns and noting them as he did so. When he reached their boat he looked confused for a moment, then said "oh, you guys." He pulled a new frame with some cable ties from his bag.

"here on the stern rail okay?"

Kate nodded. He expertly attached the frame, clipped the ends of the ties, and inserted a card, a big red "X" into the frame.

"They'll generate the map within the next hour or so. It'll pop up on your ansible."

". . . . ansible?"

"oh. . . ." he said ". . .they'll bring you one of those too." He slid a card with "D243" in the frame on *Tosca's* stern, and headed off down the row.

"Ansible?" she said to Hank.

He pulled out a book-sized lump from his cabin, bright yellow, obviously waterproof, with a palm sized screen, a thumb keyboard, and a back studded with solar cells.

"Ansible" he said "how we keep in touch."

Sandy took the thing and turned it over and over. Technology was to Sandy what boats were to Kate. "Bluetooth?" she said?

"Same frequency" said Hank.

"They must just talk to each other."

He nodded "non centered distributed network. When we're this close together, we get broadband, streaming video, phone, the works. Out further, its all packet switching. They'll bring you one."

This place, Kate thought, gets more and more interesting.

"And on that subject, I had email from Admiralty. There's a council meeting in three days, and they'll take up your crew membership then. They'll probably send somebody around to talk to you before then."

"Do we need to fill out anything or. . . . ?"

Hank just laughed. "We don't DO filling out. Anything you need?"

"We're low on supplies," said Sandy, " water especially." Hank pointed over her shoulder.

A grey haired woman, wirey in a blue jumpsuit, was unreeling an unwieldy roll of hose down the center of the docking palisade. About every three meters there was some kind of spigot.

"Potable water." said Hank, "You can run a line to your boat to fill up the tanks, but don't leave it connected. Makes uncoupling too slow if we have to break the raft in an emergency. I usually just drag my cans out and fill em there, otherwise I get water all over the damn place."

"Are there showers anywhere, or do we do that ourselves?"

"They haven't generated a map yet." Hank stood on his cabin and looked around. ". . . .but. . . .there, that blue one, that's a bathhouse. I'd go now before the map comes out, otherwise it'll be mobbed. It looks like a market next to it, the low one there. Just take a bag and take what you need. You don't need money here. You also don't need ID. If you got any questions, just ask anybody."

They grabbed their towels and toiletries, and a couple of plastic sacks.

"Will you be here Hank?" asked Kate "Do we need to lock up?"

"You never need to lock up...in fact, when we're rafting, don't. Your neighbors could need to get aboard to move or save your boat in an emergency, and if we break the raft when you're away, someone will jump aboard and pilot your boat to safety. We're family here. You never need to worry."

After a few false starts, they found the bathhouse, and after assurances from the proprietors that they didn't need to be stingy with the recycled water, they took a blasting hot shower, soaping each other up and giggling and luxuriating in the hot water. After drying off, they found the market boat, a big sailing scow, and filled their bags with fresh vegetables and a bottle of Chilean wine, and on the way back found a shrimper and returned with all the makings of a feast. They fed Hank as well, who seemed delighted.

As night fell, they sat up late under the stars, talking Fleet with Hank and getting buzzed on the wine, and when he retired, they went below decks and made love to exhaustion and fell asleep, finally, in each other's arms.

In the morning, groggy, Kate awoke and was somewhat startled to find Sandy sitting stark naked on deck.

"Look!" she said.

All around them, the raft was alive. People of all walks of life, old people and kids and parents and teens, greeting and talking and painting and working their boats, all of them seemingly happy, all of them busy, and most of them stark naked.

"This," said Sandy" is going to be a very interesting place to live."

13:   The Admiral

His name was Bobby Carlin, and his grandmother had
been an Ames and her grandfather had been an Ames
and HER grandfather had been a Boyd and his mother
had been a Bowles....as in the sister of William Augustus
Bowles, and he was soft and sensitive and romantic and
impressionable and bookish and queer and socially
hopeless and at 23 he had become the prince of a
country he'd never heard of.

It was perfect.

And from the moment the old man told him about the
Island, he had been on fire. Working ostensibly for his
college paper, he had written the first and only history
of the Island. Now he was a part of that history. The
former princes had endured some of the most
tumultuous times of history. But Bobby Carlin was a
child of the 60's, undauntable, and full of information
about solar and wind power, organic greenhousing,
alternative construction methods.....Others had
inherited the office wondering if they could deal with it.
Bobby relished the challenge.

Even before the untimely death of Johnathan III, he had abandoned his studies and plunged into research. He amassed a library on seawalls and dock construction, on alternative power and food production, on history and piracy and political systemology.
He meticulously identified groups within the U.S. and U.K. that might be interested in a homeland. He contacted hippies and yippies, psychedelecists and ceremonial magicians, witches and eco-activists and free-speechers and pacifists and communalists and free Abaco island libertarians. He had this sense of bringing all of these disparate threads together.....all of these disparate movements would come together on his wonderful, magical island and bring about a new renaissance for humanity. He was madly in love.

When Purdee died and he actually ascended the throne, he began in earnest. He lined up construction teams and equipment, he networked plans that, amazingly, all of his allies finally agreed to. He was ready. By 1980, the elements were coming together. It was only a matter of time.

He never expected America to go mad.

In 1980 Ronald Reagan swept into power on a wave of fear, conspiracy, and corruption, and the world changed. First the "war on drugs" made easy transit between islands impossible. Then the cold warriors of the Republicans forced a new maritime treaty down the throats of the U.N. Henceforth, every person, every scrap of dry land, every shallow and reef, was to be under the suzerainty of an established nation, and every nation must declare themselves under the sway of either the American or Soviet empires, or to be neutral and hence relegated to a political paralysis.

The Americans turned on the screws in the Gulf and
Caribbean. One by one, economic pressure forced island
nations to abandon their second passport and economic
citizenship programs and to tighten their ports to
service American paranoia. Finally, under pressure
from the Americans, the Bahamian government
descended on the island, were greeted as friends, and
then unceremoniously booted off all 25 of the residents,
forcing some of the elderly at gunpoint to their boats.
The new treaty ceded ALL of the Cay Sal to Bahamas,
and America was determined that they would enforce it.

Carlin went into a rage. He stewed for three days, then
hit on a plan that all concerned agreed was inspired, if
not brilliant.

He would mount a group of boats to the island, the
Bahamians not having the resources to keep it patrolled.
On the vessels would be a number of ingenious, easily
assembled buildings, including large geodesic domes,
fully equipped with solar and wind generating plants,
reverse osmosis water production plants, and, of all
things, computers. The moment this collapsable
paradise was in place, his minions would bring in the
press, supplying them with his history of Perrin Island,
touring the cool new age facilities, establishing it as a
wondrous and romantic place in a troubled world.

It was so positive, it couldn't fail.

For the six remaining months of the hurricane season,
Prince William II prepared his expedition. There were
three-frequency tensegrity domes that would auto
assemble on site. There were solar fired ammonia cycle

refrigeration systems, wind generators, solar panels, composting toilets. There was a film library, a library of great works using new microfiche technology, there were self-deploying organic greenhouses, solar distilleries for fresh water, salt reclamation units..... virtually every dime of the remaining Imperial stashes were used to create an entirely new nation, a new homeland. I would be perfect.

The Prince left from Key Largo with a fleet of ten vessels on a surprisingly warm, clear November day. The wind was from the West when they crossed the gulf stream, assuring a calm passage. At the end of the second day, they arrived.

Perrine Island was gone.

14:   Asklepius

Asklepius was an old vessel. No one remembered her
original name. She had started life as a Choy Lee Yawl,
a beautiful thing of polished wood and brass. But
sometime in the '90's she'd been clobbered in a
hurricane off Dominica and her hull had sat gathering
weeds and birdshit for over a decade until the fleet
began to gather itself and someone had notice that the
old fiberglass hull that everyone had been ignoring would
still hold water.

So she'd been cleaned out, and her ruined deckhouse
cannibalized to make four sunny cabins and a galley, and
her cable races were strung for life support gear and
O2. And so the old hull became **Asklepius**, named for
the Greek God of Healing, and became a place of refuge.
A space for the recovery of the sick and for the dying,
a way to end life in dignity.

Bess fell into the last category. She had come to the
fleet--reluctantly--with Marcus long before he became
Admiral, before it was called the Fleet. She was, as
they said, a "difficult woman," the relationship between
her and the calm of the Admiral always stormy, fire and

ice, like waves of warm and cold air mixing. The Crew had long since lost count of her lovers as they had of his, and mostly kept out of the way of her all too frequent rages.

But there was an unmistakable bond between them. She was as brilliant as was he, fiery as he was mellow, pragmatic as he was romantic, and in those moments when they clicked, people stood back and watched, amazed.

But now Iron Bess was dying, the lupus she had fought all her life finally having gotten purchase. It was rumored the Americans had a cure, but then, the Americans always claimed to have a cure, and they talked to precious few nations these days.

There were good days and bad days. This was somewhere between the two.

"How you doing, girl?"

He had asked her that virtually every day for the last two years. They both knew the drill.

"all right. I slept last night for a change. They finally got that idiot in the blue Gulfstream to turn off his fucking decklights. . ."

"I know. We shifted him next to the refrigeration ship."

She giggled. It was a sound that he didn't get to hear much anymore, and he smiled at it.

"You're bad" she said, smiling and looking at him slyly. "Seeing anyone?" She knew the answer. She knew there wasn't anyone else, no one serious. She knew, for all the grief she had given him sometimes, that there never had been.

"No time. We got way too far north this time. It was almost a problem."

"You were right. " she said " We were right to leave. The Americans are insane, as much as I've missed it. I just wanted to make sure you knew I knew that."

"I know." He kissed her. Her breath was foul. Another infection.

"Read to me?"

He did. He hit the bookseller's boats and the crew data library every week for her. Sometimes the books were data, sometimes battered paperback copies, always fiction, always history or crime stories, sci-fi or fantasy. This was a hardcopy, some battered hardcover from a series author he'd remembered she'd liked. He kept a list online, trying to keep track of what she'd read. Her vision was bad now, and the sheer fatigue of holding a book was sometimes too much for her.

He dug out his spotted glasses and found where he'd left off. He didn't mind. She'd been his right hand for thirty years. He could spare her a few hours. "I heard from Jim Silverman," he said, fiddling with the book. The pages were becoming detached, ". . .sends his regards."

She smiled again. "I always liked them. How's Maggie?"

"Didn't say. It was just a note." Maggie had been gone for years. She was forgetting lately.

He read for about an hour and a half before she drifted off. She looked fine when she was attentive or chatting, but asleep, she looked sunken, the flesh pooling off her bones. He looked at her sadly. "Oh, baby. . . ." He tucked the book in her bedside table for next time.

"She loves it when you come" said the orderly as he left.

"I'll check in this evening." He tried to smile. He wasn't good a losing.

The raft undulated slowly in the calming waters. The breeze was warm and friendly. People smiled and waved. His people. His crew. His family. He had come out here over a decade ago, an aging eccentric and his reluctant mate and his little boat. He had played the game, dropping his name and becoming "Marcus." Maybe a year, he had said, maybe two years, just until things settle down in the States.

But things had never settled down. America had broken, with half the states in a defacto alliance with Canada and Europe and the rest degenerating into a kind of insane militarism.

And the Fleet, the gathering of burners and iconoclasts and pagans and anarchists and artists....all of them, oddly, had actually listened to him. And even odder, some of his ideas had actually worked. So now he *was* Marcus, Admiral of the Fleet, warm in the bosom of his nation and community, and at the same time more alone than he'd ever been.

He took some time to himself. If they needed him someone would find him. He walked the gangways in the warm evening, accepting a nosh here, a glass of rum there. It was pleasant at least. There were more boats every day, more he didn't know, and the Fleet was growing and growing and growing. Here were two new Sharpies he'd never seen before, and one ragged looking gigantic sloop scow, here was a new seaplane, here was a beautiful little Weekender tied next to Hank's tortuga.
. . . .

The stars were out by the time he pulled himself back aboard **Dragonfly**. There were, mercifully, no messages. He poured himself a glass of chilled white wine, something Martin had given him, dry and redolent of apples and cinnamon. Tomorrow was the Council meeting, and the morning would be filled with discussions with his officers. More shit to deal with, more details.

And then there was the unshakable feeling that something was coming. He could feel it like the pressure before a storm, something of promise and threat, a nexus, a place of memetic pivot the Verlainists would have said.

If he just could get a break, he thought, just a little peace. . . .

Then he heard Bess' voice in his head, dry like the rustle of leaves, full of wry laughter, saying: "When the fuck have you ever wanted peace and quiet?"

He smiled and killed the last of the wine and the lights.

Okay, Bessie. Okay....

15:   The Fleet

Carlin had them check the location again and again. He
sent divers down. Where Perrin island had once stood
was a ten metre gouge in the coral floor of the Gulf.
The Americans, the fucking Americans, at the
"request" of the Bahamian government, had simply
come and dynamited the place.

And there was nothing for it. The shallows that had
contained the Island were the only space outside the
escarpment of the Cay Sal bank that could support an
island, all else was Bahamian territory, jealously
patrolled by the Americans as a courtesy. They drifted
for three days. Then, without a word, his men headed
the ships back home.

Most of the Islanders and the amalgamation of groups
he'd assembled drifted away. They had their own lives,
their own fish to fry. Some of the contraptions were
sold off, some went into storage. For three years,
Carlin tried to make it work. He tried to find other
spaces, other shallows. He tried to buy islands, to bribe
governments into hosting the Empire, to find ways to
use drilling platforms, sea walls, anything. . . .It was

useless. No one wanted the trouble the Islanders would bring during the cold war, and as the Soviet Union began to wind down, it just got worse. The Americans were looking for an enemy, ANY enemy, a new "evil empire" to justify themselves, and nobody wanted to be "it".

Then there were the disturbing hydrological papers he'd been getting. There was no disguising it, sea levels were rising, and the seas were warming. All that meant SERIOUS trouble for any small island, and doubly so for any artificial dredge and fill construct not being bolstered by natural accretion.

Worse than any of this, he felt as if he'd let the old man down, him and all the Islanders and all the history of the place. It all just sucked.

Bobbie Carlin went off the deep end. He headed back to college, washed out, went on a major bender, totaled his car. His obsession alienated his friends and, frankly, scared the remaining Island loyalists, who began to wonder if Johnathan III hadn't made a mistake in his successor. It all just sucked.

He found himself sitting on a dock in Hampton Rodes in the middle of the night, feeling like crap, rehashing the whole thing over and over in his mind. The whole Island thing just seemed undoable, unrepeatable. Buy or build an island was just to create a target for the Americans and for the weather, two forces that were damn near unstoppable at this point.

The idea, when it came, nearly knocked him off the dock.

"Why, "said William II, "do I need an Island?"

16:   Pensacola

When the base's chief weather officer walked into Vice Admiral Silverman's office, Silverman knew something was up. Capt. Kelly had served with him for five years, and was generally regarded as a wizard when it came to all things meteorological.

But when he walked through the door with a sheaf of brown folders and that look on his face. . . .

Capt. Kelly touched his finger to his lips before Jim Silverman could say a word. They all knew, the walls had ears.

"Admiral, I thought if you were free, I could take you out to see the new doppler station on Santa Rosa, maybe catch lunch on the way."

Silverman *wasn't* free, but he was about to *get* himself free.

"Good Idea, Captain, I've been meaning to. Shall we ask Captain Spall if he'd like to join us?"

Spall was Silverman's quartermaster, and an ally.

"Sure." said Kelly, with a brightness that utterly belied his expressions. "I got my kid's car today, the Mustang. Thought you might enjoy that."

Riding in an un-airconditioned '60's gas guzzler was about the last thing on Silverman's list. But no navy car meant no navy tracers and no navy bugs and WHAT was Kelly up to?

"Great." said Silverman, trying to be enthusiastic. Spoke to his aide and moved a few things around, they picked up Spall on the way out of the building, and left.

Still, they spoke of nothing until they were off base. Ever conscious of the degree of scrutiny going on these days. Once they were on the road to the island, Kelly passed out his folders. Pages of maps and charts, graphs and tables, water temperatures, wind, sea levels, wave heights. . . . .these were career sailors. They lived and breathed this stuff.

They ate lunch at an outdoor cafe on the beach. Careful to speak of nothing, being careful to be seen as what they should appear to be, conscious of the fact that they had, indeed, been followed: two SP's and a civilian-- most likely a political compliance officer or maybe Homeland Security--who kept a discrete distance.

After lunch they headed down the island, through the crumbling brick ruin of Ft. Pickens to the new Naval Reserve and it's high-tech laser doppler weather setup. By this time they were done talking. . . quiet. . .taciturn. They did a cursory inspection for the security cameras and left.

Back at base, Silverman canceled his afternoon appointments and told his aide: "Get me the Secretary on a secured line. Tell him it's personal, but I may have an extraordinary request of him. THAT should get him to call us back."

Then Vice Admiral Jas. Silverman went back to his office, sat at his desk, and practiced being very very still.

17:   The End of Empire

The idea was so simple. For most of the Island's
history, most of its inhabitants had lived on boats. The
few buildings of the island were civic ones, homes for
the ruling family, mostly just showpieces. Boats
weren't like buildings on stilts. Boats could move. They
could move out of the way of storms, and the new
weather satellites would show them where to go. Boats
could avoid trouble spots, could disperse if things got
nasty, fragmenting into a hundred different units and
providing no target for the huge navy's of the great
empires. Then they could quietly, simply reassemble
themselves, and get on with life.

Even better, most of the gizmos he'd been so excited
about could be mounted on boats as well as marine
platforms, and he still HAD most of his gizmos.

Better and better.

The fleet of ships would need weapons to defend
themselves minimally....he could design those, those
could be built. They would need communications and
food supply vessels and floating greenhouses and water

desalination units....ditto. They would need sustainable vessel designs, ways of rafting in calm water, ways of navigating. . . .all doable.

The problem, he realized in a flash, was governance. Johnathan III had run into the edges of it decades earlier with the New Hebrides pilgrims. As romantic as the empire was, people were just plain sick of being pushed around. Even the supposed democracies were being run by monied elite, the new aristocrats, and the wrangling of parties and interest groups and big money and corruption was bleeding the life out of people. On top of that, this new fleet would have to be able to function in a decentralized fashion. Breaking apart and recombining wouldn't support a top-down monarchic management.

He stopped the boozing and hanging out at drag clubs. He buried himself in his books. He read Plato and Marx, he read Jefferson and Heinlein and James. He read Bucky Fuller and Chapelle and Bolger and Sirius and Hoffmann. He made drawing after drawing after drawing, teaching himself draftsmanship in the process. He typed reams. Finally, after five months, he spent his last $278 on bus tickets and long distance calls.

In a disused ballroom at a moldering yacht club in Georgia, he spread out his plans to a room of Islanders and others that still held a modicum of interest....at least, those he could interest enough to come. They listened respectfully. The ideas were novel, clever, and surprisingly detailed. He outlined how a fleet could sail in a cycle, rafting much of the time, that would avoid storms and national boundaries, cycling through the Gulf, Atlantic, and Caribbean as it did so, trading with islands and servicing vacationers, scientists, and travelers. He offered detailed designs for service ships, patrol vessels, public spaces, food production boats. . . . He covered everything coverable, and they were impressed, he could see. They realized that it could be done. . . .

. . . provided you still wanted to do that sort of thing. But he could see it in their eyes: why should I do this? Why should I leave my tolerable life to follow *you*?

And then Carlin dropped his bomb. "You would not follow me. I would abdicate. I would end the empire forever."

You could've heard a human hair hit the floor.

"The time," Carlin went on, " for this monarchy thing is long over. It worked for the 19th century, but we're moving into the 21st now, and it's done. I have a new proposal."

And he dug out the rest of his charts.

His new governance was based on something old: it followed the ships articles of 17th century pirate vessels, which fit with the piratical history of the Islanders nicely. Like those ships, the captain of this new band--the admiral of the fleet, really--would be elected, and would serve as more city manager than potentate. In fact, all of the officers would be chosen by a council of the fleet and would serve at their suffrage. To avoid politics, the governing council would be chosen by lot every year from the crew of the fleet, a method borrowed from classical Athenian government. To avoid corruption, all the members of the fleet had access to all the services and goods of the fleet, just as a ship's crew can depend on the ship's services. The story he spun was romantic and pragmatic, a floating 60's commune with a piratical edge. They saw it. They saw themselves living on the boats, living as a pirate crew, but with modern day amenities. Some of them saw their worries about debts and medical care evaporating. Some of them saw their longing for the sea sated. Some of them saw it as a future.

And, of course, some did not. They wished him luck. Some made donations of money or boats.

But at the end of the day, 23 vessels joined the fleet, with many more to follow.

So Bobby Carlin, a young, bookish, gay man who became William II of the Perrine Muscogee, ended the empire of the island forever, and the fleet was born.

18:   The Council

It was just exactly as Kate had pictured it, just the way her father had described. Within the raft were a series of floating "squares," really little more than spaces where floating dock was tied to floating dock and covered with a sunshade to make some semblance of public space. There were several of these, all identical from the air. But only one each rafting was designated the Agora, only one was where the Council stood, and this time, this one was it.

Beneath the broad canvas tarp stood two makeshift tables, nothing more than rough beams laid across barrels (she learned later the wooden barrels were fakes, designed to nest and break down. This was for effect. Who the hell uses wooden barrels anymore, anyway?). One table was laid out in a broad horseshoe, and set with 12 rough wooden chairs, one for each of the 12 Councilors, with a bench behind and to the right of each for their vice counsels. Embraced by the horseshoe was another straight trestle table, set for the officers.

Two crew members were setting up, pens and paper at

each place, but these were quill pens, and the paper was parchment. Her father had once said that all government was theatre, was a kind of collective identity for the nation served. The English were yeomen, the Cubanos were revolutionaries, the Americans were....well...insane. The Fleet were pirates and Renegados.

In the place where the Admiral would sit was a glass case with a rusting cutlass. Apparently someone had realized the Fleet's only relic was going to disintegrate if they didn't do something to protect it from the sea air. A cannonball stood in a small brass base, a stand-in for a gavel.

Theatre.

Once each year, on the first of May, the Fleet held a lottery. Twelve crewmen's names were drawn at random by a child, and they became the defacto rulers of the fleet, serving a year as vice counsel, learning the ropes, and then a year as a full member of the council. The council was legislature and judiciary. It was a body designed to represent the crew, a governmental form descended from the ship's articles of Piracy's Golden Age, an ancient agreement designed to avoid politics, to make factions difficult.

The Officers, the Admiral, Quartermaster, Bosun, and their subordinates, served at the Council's pleasure, served for only so long as the Council was pleased with them.

Theatre.

The Fleet's governance was neither ancient nor

traditional. It had been created by the Admiral's predecessor, the legendary Admiral Carlin, who had ended the monarchic pretensions of the Fleet rulers. Admiral Marcus had continued the work, shepherding the Fleet through its unexpected growth and attendant political complications.

Theatre.

They had gotten as much information as they could, Kate and Sandy. They had found out from Hank how to dress, how to stand. . . .be yourselves, he had said, but respectful. Be forceful and sure, he had said, but respectful. Know who you are, know what your worth is. Kate had chosen simple denim. Who she was. And boat sandals. Sandy had goth'd herself out, black dress, and alluring. Hank had just smiled.

At some signal Kate didn't track, the council filed in. They seemed to come from every direction at once, each seat accompanied by a vice counselor. They had dressed, each in their own way, an oddball mix of modern dress and late 17th century kitsch. Each of the vice Counselors carried a leather valise, papers and an ansible. That must be how the cued this.
They took their places, shuffling papers.

"Officers on Deck!"

And everyone was on their feet.

And the Pirates came.

From three directions came the three coequal Officers of the fleet and their retinues, all in full 17th century drag except for the ubiquitous Fleet carbines and disguised ansibles. The officers took their places at the table, with their subordinates taking up places behind them.

It was the Admiral she couldn't take her eyes off of. She had seen him around the raft, Hank had pointed him out. But this was different. He was in his place. She stared at him. Admiral Marcus was every inch the pirate, greying hair past his shoulders, a grey muzzle, and radiating power. . . .right now at least. Suddenly she knew. Her dad. He reminded her of her dad.

Theatre

The Admiral struck the cannonball three times against it's base.

"Members of the council, by your orders we convene this meeting."

The Council sat first, the Officers waiting respectfully until they did so. The message was clear: We work for you.

The meeting itself was far from exciting. This was the day to day functioning of a working government, the Officers serving like city managers for the Fleet. Kate stood in the heat, sweat trickling down her neck, and wondered how the Officers stood their outfits.

And then the Vice Counsel for the first seat said: "And now to the matter of new Crew members..."

The Admiral turned to the Quartermaster. "How many have applied this time?"

"Eighteen"

"And of those how many do we bring forward?"

The Quartermaster smiled. "Two".

And way too many sets of eyes turned toward Kate and Sandy.

"We're on" Sandy said under her breath.

"let them come forward" said Admiral Marcus.

Kate swallowed hard and the two of them came to stand before the council. Strong, but respectful, Kate kept saying to herself, strong but respectful....

"You are of the *Ganymeade*?" Said the Admiral.

"We are." they said in unison.

"How came you by the ship?" Again, a formality.

"I built her," said Kate, "along with my late father."

The officers nodded. "How would you be known to the fleet?" said the Quartermaster, barely looking up from her notes. They were ready for this one. Everyone took a Fleet name on joining the crew.

"This is Cat. " Said Sandy, "I"m Natasha..."

"She looks like a Natasha." Muttered the Navigator. Natasha/Sandy looked at him from beneath her bangs, trying to appear dangerous.

The Admiral ignored him. "Why have you come here with your vessel?"

"To sign the Articles and join the Fleet."

The Admiral looked at Sandy. "And you come with her, of your own free will?" Sandy nodded. "I do." Kate felt like they had just gotten married.

"What do you bring to the fleet? "said the Bosun, "what skills?"

"Chandlery, " said Kate, " woodwork and maintenance. You've only to look at the woodwork on my boat to see our skills."

"We toured your vessel before this meeting," said the Bosun. Kate wondered suddenly where her underpants had wound up. "It's Bristol." he concluded,"one of the best kept I've seen. You can work wood, the two of you, and handle glass."

The Admiral looked dead at them. "Why did you come here? Why here? Why now?"

"To be free. "said Sandy, " to find our destiny."

"You're Americans," said the Admiral, " What couldn't you do there that we would tolerate you doing here? What is it you need to do?"

Kate hesitated. This wasn't in the script. She had this awful sense of things going amiss, of their membership hanging by her next words. . .

. . .but it was Sandy that answered. Sandy grabbed her and kissed her full on the mouth. She took her time. It was a moment before Kate caught on and relaxed. Then they both took their time. The Council laughed and applauded. "Point Taken," said the Admiral, smiling. "How say you Master Constable?" The Constable stood from his place behind the Quartermaster, a giant of a man, Ansible in hand.

Hank. . . .they hadn't a clue.

"Officers, neither of these two have any warrants outstanding, nor do they seem to comprise a risk to the fleet. Natasha has skillfully seeded the rumor that she has run off with a boyfriend in the service--nicely done, madam--and is unlikely to be sought after. Cat's stepfather is a politico with the Americans and has been making hay out of her disappearance. Our contacts believe he is in no real hurry to find her, and that the fleet is unlikely to be implicated. No downside, either way. Both have impeccable academic records and are well thought of in their communities and are likely to be an asset to the fleet. Then, Admiral Marcus, there is this matter." Hank handed his ansible to the Admiral.

The Admiral perused the ansible's little screen, looking up from it at them periodically. It was hard to tell but he seemed to be looking at Kate. Finally he handed back the ansible and leaned back in his seat.

"Cat, your natural father was Robert Beaumont?"

"Aye sir."

". . .a naval aviator?"

"He was once, yessir."

"And his middle name?"

What was going on? "Ferrin, sir, after his grandfather."

"I'll be damned." said the Admiral "Bob Beaumont........"He looked up suddenly, struck the cannonball once on its base, and declared:" Legacy, and spouse.......! Next issue."

Hank shooed them out as the council took up other matters.

Kate was confused. She asked Hank what had just happened.

"Your father was fleet. As his daughter you and your spouse have the right to join. It's a legacy, and one of the few times I've seen it invoked. You're fleet, the both of you. Congratulations. "

And then Sandy was around her neck and bouncing up and down, and they both hugged and kissed Hank....what they could reach of him...and laughed. The rest of the day was a blur. They had to read aloud and sign the articles, they signed the bone tiles that would be used in the Council lottery, their signatures would later be scrimshawed into the pieces. Every boat they passed seemed to know, and there was food and wine and hugs and kisses and gifts and when they finally reeled back to *Ganymeade* at sunset, Sandy had her dress off before she hit the rail and dragged Kate below decks.

That night, as she slept, she had a dream. She had awakened on the boat in Sandy's sleeping arms and had crept on deck in the night to find her father sitting on the dock, grinning at her and swishing his feet boyishly in the water.

"You planned this, didn't you?" she said to him fondly.

"I know you. I knew you might need an out. I knew you were smart enough to take it. "

"I miss you daddy." she said, smiling, but feeling the tears on her face.

"I never left." he said "You'll wake up in the morning as Cat of the Ganymeade with a whole life ahead of you, and I couldn't be happier. I'll be there all the time, honey. You only have to look around. Love you, sweetheart. I'm here all the time, all the time you need me. I'm so happy for you."

And he slipped beneath the waters, smiling.

19:   Carlin's Fleet

If William II--little Bobby Carlin--had any weakness, it was also his strength: his passion for organization. Carlin was a list maker and chart drawer, a simulation runner of obsessive intensity. "The kid," Bill Cunningham once wrote ,"is the poster child for game theory." Still, you can't plan on everything. When Carlin's overequipped little fleet left port, there were too many of some supplies, not enough of others. The varying hull speeds of the boats meant that keeping the group together was an absolute nightmare, and the inability to accurately predict the fleet's speed sent them right through the middle of a tropical storm instead of around it like they'd intended. Still, even though they'd had to put into Long Key for repairs, they were feeling pretty good about themselves, and some of the former fellow travelers, seeing the fleet in the water, had decided to make the jump and join in as well.

By the time the fleet had its first rafting in the Nicholas Channel, there were 42 vessels with 106 adults as members of the crew. The rafting went smoother than anyone had dreamed, with Carlin's rafting plank idea binding the ships together and creating walkways and public spaces. The water distribution system worked. The power distribution system worked. Mercifully, the sanitation system worked. They celebrated. They ate and drank together, with emphasis on the drinking. It was time for the crew to choose it's first council.

Which of course caused the first problems.

Carlin had planned a government that he'd hoped would avoid the rankling, partisanship, and corruption he had seen during the slow, painful collapse of the American republic. His Council would be chosen at random from the citizens, and all the citizens, the "crewmembers" could draw on the fleet's resources for the necessities of life, hopefully eliminating some of the need for greed and gain and corruption. The Council would then decide on the officers, who would serve at their suffrage and for as long as their service was competent.

He had worked out a lovely little waltz of ritual wherein each of the crew members would sign the articles, their names would be dropped into a bowl, and the names of the first council chosen.

Therein lay the sticking points. Very few of the crew wanted to sign ANYthing. If this enterprise didn't work or if they got tired of it, most wanted the option of returning to their old lives without facing the retribution of the increasingly-nasty US government. Then there was the matter of just WHO should draw the names. Carlin had intended it to be the Admiral (that would be him), but the crew was suspicious. What's to stop a little slight of hand from happening with the drawing, they asked.

After much discussion and a LOT more drinking, a

solution emerged....no one remembers who suggested it. The crew could take "fleet names" for purposes of membership (usually tagged with the name of the vessel on which they sailed to avoid confusion). Just as Bobby Carlin became William II, so your average Joe Smith could become Crabclaw of the **Oargasm** within the fleet. It was kind of like being in the old French Foreign Legion, a way to wipe the slate clean and start over. As for the lottery, someone finally yelled out "let the twerp do it." The "twerp" in this case was the hyperactive four year old daughter of one of the crewmembers who, like the rest of the children, had spent most of the rafting pounding back and forth on the rafting planks--happy to be out of the cramped sailboats--usually stark naked.

So it was that the crew of the Fleet signed the first set of Articles, along with a parchment slip with their crew name and vessel. The slips were laid out under a sheet of plastic so that everyone could be sure every name that should be there WAS there, then they were dumped into a cracked glass fishbowl and the "twerp," (later Cyndi of the *Maitland*) with surprising solemnity chose the first 12 Councilors and the first 12 vice Councilors. The Council, now firmly drunk on their asses, unanimously chose Carlin as the first Admiral, followed, after some shuffling, with a full slate of officers.

Then the drinking started in earnest.

When the dawn broke the next morning, the crew awoke hung over, mostly naked, often with inappropriate partners, and firmly as a nation.

Over the next few months, as the Fleet completed its first "cycle" of the Gulf and Caribbean, the Council proved itself, as did the continuing genius and inventiveness of Admiral Carlin. When keeping the fleet together became a problem, he cobbled together remotely piloted vehicles and video balloons to give them a panoramic view of their own dispersal. When small boats of armed men off Haiti menaced the raft, Carlin took advantage of the sea of cheap old Soviet ammunition then washing the planet and had his machine shop crank out simplified knockoffs of the 1931 Finnish Soumi 31 machine carbine to beef up their own protection (the ubiquitous "fleet carbine", its plans stuck by someone on the internet, was to become the staple of liberation movements worldwide for a generation). He authored and coordinated the Fleet's first educational system, its first meteorological center, its first data library. . .

Nor were the crewmembers slackers when it came to innovation. They looked at what they needed, they looked at the lives they wanted, and they built. They built cafes and theatres, they created markets and shower facilities and drydocks and gardens, they created a life.

By the time the Fleet began it's second "cycle" the word had gotten out. Curious cruisers came to join the raft to experience the crew 'experience'. Carlin charged them a nominal dockage fee, in euros or dollars, then used the money for more supplies. Some fell in love with the lifestyle and dumped their resources into the fleet, growing it in number and in wealth. By the end of the cycle, Carlin was forced to design fast patrol craft to steer the curious to appropriate dockage (and to make sure they weren't coming with ill intent) and created the first of the "Vesper" class of sharpies. Drunks, two attempted rapes, a robbery, and one looney-tunes attempted takeover caused the rapid expansion of the constabulary under the office of the Quartermaster. By the end of the third cycle, the Fleet was nearly 700 vessels, over 1700 crewmembers, five radio stations, two television stations, and 135 bars. Still, trade came hard. No one recognized the fleet's passports, and ships were forced to change colors and use American or Commonwealth passports to come into ports for supplies.

Ironically, it was a storm that bought the Fleet a modicum of respectability. On the Fleet's seventh cycle, right at the tag end of the storm season, a small, very fast hurricane had clobbered Guadeloupe and Dominica, and Admiral Carlin had offered some of the excess facilities he still was towing in storage to help. With permission of the Dominican government, a small flotilla had come into Prince Rupert Bay and up the mouth of the Indian River. The Crew members ran powerlines ashore, provided a water station for the citizens of ruined Portsmouth, and had forged ashore with tools, tarps, and temporary structures, including many of the self assembling domes that Carlin had been dragging along for a decade. A smaller group of Crewmembers set up a field clinic in St. Barths, at Gustavia. While their former colonial parents dithered and the Americans beat the drum of how much they would be giving--donations that would only go to US companies to rebuild their own overseas subsidiaries-- the Fleet was actually on the ground and helping folks. Dominica recognized the fleet outright. The French overseas office and the Dutch government on St. Maartins quietly concluded mutual assistance agreements. The Cubans, always happy to anger the Yankees, recognized them as well. The Fleet, in an astonishingly short time, was becoming more than just a curiosity.

Admiral Carlin's remarkable tenure with the fleet was not to be long lived. In the spring of his fifth season as Admiral he suffered a mild heart attack. Ignoring the advice of his doctor and friends, he refused to slow down, keeping up the dizzy pace of work he'd always subscribed to. Two months later, he was found dead in his cockpit, a page of elaborate notes still in his hand.

His burial at sea, just south of Grand Cayman, was attended by emissaries of many of the Caribbean states. With his passing, the connection with William Bowles, the Foote Princes, and much of the past ended. The future was now a blank slate.

Carlin was succeeded, on second vote of the Council, by his far more steady Quartermaster, Marcus of the **Dragonfly**. Marcus was regarded as a good man by most--steady, though far short of the brilliance they'd seen in Carlin--but his irritating wife grated a lot of the crew the wrong way. They had no idea how well they'd chosen.

The Fleet continued to grow by leaps and bounds, a kind of punctuated equilibrium driven mostly by the increasing insanity of the American government. The U. S. invasion of Bolivia brought a surge of refugees and anti-war protesters. The banning of the 30-year old Burning Man festival in Nevada "and other associated events not in keeping with Christian Family Values" brought yet another surge of Burners and their equipment and their iconoclastic, can-do attitude. The "Christian Nation" act brought scads of atheists and agnostics and Neo-Pagans and those just plain sick of what America was becoming.

On the morning of the Fleets 100th rafting, Admiral Marcus looked at the raft map he had just been presented by the Quartermaster. The thing looked like a circuit board.

"How many?" asked Admiral Marcus.

"27,221 separate vessels," said the Quartermaster, "not counting our patrol boats."

"And crewmembers?" said the Admiral.

"62,580, counting the two we'll bring on at the council today." said the Quartermaster.

"....not counting kids, refugees, tourists, and assorted hangers on...."said Marcus.

"Its over 100,000 people, Admiral, all told."

"That's twice the population of most of these islands......Is it too early, " said Admiral Marcus, "for me to start drinking?"

The Quartermaster just grinned at him. She'd come to know his moods.

"As my daddy usta tell me, " she said " it's always five o'clock somewhere."

20:   Home In The Fleet

The fleet was a wonder, pure and simple. The raft was
a patchwork small town community that had grown into
a chaotic city, each vessel at once home and business,
all done, not for money, but for love. "The Aim"
Admiral Carlin had once said, " is to create a life that is
all about the joy we build for other people." It was an
infectious philosophy, carried to the fleet by the
Burners and SecondLifers, and it set the tone for their
lives.

So each of the boats in the crazy quilt of the raft
represented the owner's passion, from music to food,
from clothing to literature, from sex to gaming to
fishing to needlepoint, all shared openly and without
precondition, for as long during the day as the owner
chose to share it. When the fleet had a need, someone
would usually step up and fill it. Those things that no
one chose to fill the Council would fill, requiring only a
few hours from the crew members for the more
onerous jobs until someone became fascinated enough
with, say, waste disposal to take it over as a passion.
No money changed hands between members of the fleet,
not ever.

Only tourists paid, and that tourism, along with trade and media and ship's services, comprised the "business" of the fleet. Business that fed them and kept them afloat. Business with the outside world, not the internal one. The inside world was family.

Days were easy and full. Cat and Natasha--and that is what everyone called them--the "girls from *Ganymeade*," would awake happily in each others arms, snag towels and toiletries, and stroll in the buff down to the bathhouse boat (one learns, exposed to salt spray 24/7, to rinse off as often as possible), taking long hot showers together or soaking in the tubs. They would find a breakfast at one of the little cafes, explore, swim, chat with new friends. . . .they would tend the boat together, watch the sunsets together, spend long hours laughing and drinking red wine and espresso in the coffeehouses. . . .they would make elaborate meals for their friends and neighbors and attend equally elaborate meals on other boats. . . .they would swim and fish and make love on long, golden afternoons. They were deliriously happy.

Soon enough they began to serve their tithe, their service to the fleet. Cat had always assumed that the two of them would work together doing ship maintenance and cleaning, but it didn't play out like that. During an impromptu session of target practice for the Constabulary, Hank had handed a carbine to Cat--half in jest--and then watch slack jawed as she out shot most of his officers. He had recruited her on the spot. For her part, Natasha had fallen in with a gaggle of school kids and wound up teaching. Natasha was maternal. Who would've thought?

The arrangement was perfect. It gave them just the right amount of time apart, just the right number of stories to tell each other.

And one evening, facing yet another startling sunset, Cat turned to find tears streaming down Natasha's cheeks.

What's wrong?

Natasha just smiled at her, face streaming. "Happiness, " she said". . .it's possible. I never knew."

And they sat holding one another for a very long time, until long after the sun had set, until long after the stars had taken over the sky.

21.   The Secretary

Interpol Document
Secretary Ginwold Eyes Only

Received from Interpol, Bussels, gmt 09:56

Mr. Secretary,
The attached is a preliminary Interpol report based on
our investigative request supplied by us by our sources
in Brussels. This document has been leaked to the
European press. Thought you would like to know.
Robert Tiffin
Homeland Security

attached document portion begins

In other matters, regarding the two accusations
forwarded by Mr. James Arleighe, the U. S. envoy:

In the matter of child pornography and abuse in The
Fleet: the instance cited is atypical, resulting from a
young woman having been granted emancipated minor
status within the Fleet to care for an ailing parent (it
must be noted that the U.S. has similar laws, though the

Fleet versions are more comprehensive). Prior to her reaching majority as considered by the fleet she produced a series of provocative digital images which were sold to Americans touring the Carribean. It must be noted that her age at the time of these photos would have been considered legal thoughout most of South America and Africa, and would have been on or above the age of consent in four of the American States, each of which have their own laws regarding this. As this was a single incedent, the legality of which is hazy internationally at best, and clearly not representing a pattern of abuse or an industry of pornographic production, the Council has denied the request for investigation.

In the matter of Fleet transfer of weapons to Terrorist groups: Since the publication over a decade ago of the plans for the "Fleet Carbine" on the internet, the weapon has become easily as common as the AK-47 and its decendants became in the last century, and no direct connection to arms sales or shipments has ever been made between non governmental armed groups and the government of the Fleet. Actual Fleet carbines, utilizing the H&K 7mm X 34mm caseless round, are only produced in two places on the planet: the Fleet itself and the Republic of China (Taiwan) under contract. None of these weapons have ever appeared in the Bolivian conflict as asserted. The presence of Type II Fleet Carbines in the pirate raid in Singapore last August was traced to a theft at the Han Shin factory on Taiwan four months earlier, and involved only three weapons, all of which were recovered. Accordingly, the Council has denied further investigation.

This is the fifth time the U. S. envoy has come forward with rather thinly researched claims against the Fleet.

The Council has seen fit to send to the United States Government Office of the Secretary of State (The Hon. Mr. Otis Barner) a letter of complaint for forwarding what are seen as thinly veiled political attacks to this office for purposes of international publicity.

attached document ends

Secretary of Defense Ginwold fumed. The damned Euorpeans. If those pussies would just fucking play ball, Ginwold could get the President, the Party, and the Press all off of his back and the Fleet out of his hair. A year and a half ago, the President himself had ask Ginwold to find something--anything--to publicly justify action against that cycling swamp of leftist perverts. Now with this bleeding to the world press and his own security people telling him an attack this spring would be "expensive in terms of casualties, and doubtful in terms of success" Ginwold was feeling frustrated. He supressed a desire to backhand his computer display, snarled at his secretary for coffee, and turned to his growing "to do" list.

Despite this, and despite his horrible mood, Secretary of Defense Ginwold got back to Jas. Silverman with astonishing promptness.

Let me qualify that.

It took almost two days for his staff to let the Secretary know that Silverman had called and had requested a response. There was then a three day period while his staff researched the political, religious, and social affiliations of the Vice Admiral, along with comments on his service record, and weighed the political costs and benefits of being associated with him. Then the Secretary's private secretary went through all known prior conversations to try to get the Secretary on top on whatever it might be that the Vice Admiral was calling him about.

So ten days after Jas Silverman had called him on this urgent matter, the Secretary of Defense, his butt now adequately covered, his coffee cup filled, and his blood pressure back down to what was, for him, near normal, finally called him back.

Silverman had expected the delay. It had given him time to prepare.

"Mr. Secretary"

"James, "said Secretary Ginwold, "how good to hear from you."

Silverman NEVER went by James.

"Good to hear from you too, sir. Thank you for getting back to me."

"Happy to do so, Admiral. What can we help you with?"

"Mr. Secretary, I've a bit of a family crisis looming, but I've realized that it might actually help us get some of the proof we need regarding The Fleet."

'Some of the proof we need' was this administration's favorite phrase. It meant supplying them with the political cover for covert operations, wiretaps, kidnappings, torture, bombing campaigns, invasions, or any other piece of "the agenda" on which they'd already decided. The Secretary was interested.

"I'm listening, James."

Silverman's tale was simple. His dear, beloved cousin Bess was dying. They had been raised together as kids in rural New Hampshire all those many years ago, and had been close until she had fallen into bad company and he had joined the service of his nation. Now she was dying, and, coincidentally, was also the wife of the Admiral of the The Fleet. The gullible, corrupt rulers of the fleet would be easily persuaded to let Vice Admiral Jas. Silverman in to visit his beloved cousin one last time. In the process, he could garner important information to give the administration (wait for it) the "Proof It Needed" to act against the clear and present danger to American interests that was the Feet.

"We have a pretty good idea that our agents in the Fleet are being fed misinformation, Mr. Secretary. This just seemed too good an opportunity to pass on."

"You'd be taking an awful risk." said the Secretary, having already decided that anything that could happen to Silverman would represent a win-win situation. Come back with information, they win. Get killed by the fanatics in the fleet, they win. . . .and maybe, just maybe, come back with nothing and a horrible accident could be blamed on the fleet just as well.

"I know, sir.   I think it's worth it."

"I appreciate your bravery, Admiral. Let me get back to you." But Ginwold was already motioning to his aide to put the wheels in motion.

"Please do, Mr. Secretary," said Silverman, knowing he had won "we may not have much time."

The Secretary hung up, cracked his knuckles, and settled back, feeling wonderfully satisfied. Maybe this time, he thought. Yes, maybe we have them this time.

Dangerous, dangerous fucking game, thought Silverman as he hung up his phone. Now if Fleet Admiral Marcus will just understand that this needs to happen, will just understand what I'm up to.

Silverman allowed himself a quiet moment, slowed his breathing, slowed his heart, then launched back into his files. This was going to be one awful fucking nightmare of a year.

22.   Admiral Marcus

The man who would become Marcus of the **Dragonfly**
hardly had a past that would have indicated his
ascention to the rank of Admiral. Bill Halliwell had been
born to a single teenage mother living in a small tourist
town on the Chesapeake's eastern shore, and had grown
up through a singularly unprepossing childhood: fishing
and reading to excess and in general keeping to himself.
His loving, struggling mother needed him to be self
sufficient. With no real education and working 60 hours
a week of minimum wage jobs to make ends meet, she
gave him the time and love she could: seiges of time
apart where he played latchkey kid separated by spells
of aching closeness when she could get off or when she
was laid off. Bill loved his mom. Loved her with a
possessive intensity that probably, in retrospect, made
her finding another relationship difficult if not
impossible.

An indifferent student, and utterly lacking in funds, Billy
Halliwell wound up attending a local community college--
usually attending class when he got around to it--and
then going out of inertia to one of the Maryland public
colleges, racking up huge college loans in the process.

Through most of it he remained as he had been: bookish, insular, and utterly self-absorbed.

That all changed when he ran into Jim Silverman.

Silverman was a local hero. He was the star player on any number of sports teams, a student on Dean's list for most of his life, and the center of the "popular" portion of college society. The only son of a wealthy and powerful New England family, his only rebellion had been his 'addiction' to aviation, which flew in the face of the family's long history of producing judges and politicians. He had come to Maryland on a sports scholarship, mostly to be near the engineers of Lockheed Martin and had quietly and skillfully shifted his major to aviation by enrolling in AFROTC, convincing his family that a "military background" as an air force officer be a plus for politics.

Thus is was that Silverman, a man born with a silver steam shovel in his mouth, star of the college, utterly sure of his supiority, came to stop by the crowded college pub for a beer prior to meeting some friends for an evening of clubbing and adulation, and found himself sitting across from Bill Halliwell.

"I had always looked down on them," said Silverman, " the geeks, the gamers, the renfaire clowns. . . .I had always considered them scruffy and hopeless, and hopelessly beneath me. I was just being polite with him, him sitting there in a stack of books and scribbling on a yellow legal pad. I ask what he was doing, and he says he's writing a short story, and that it's set in ancient Etruria or something, and that it's a pain because the only really good book he can find for background is in Italian. You read Italian I say? And he says he didn't, but since he couldn't find a translation, he had to teach himself. Ten minutes into the conversation, I'm thinking: Here's this guy, this kind of person I've always looked down on, and thanks to people like me, he thinks of himself as a waste and a loser and a failure and a joke, and I'm sitting across from this person who has a level of intellect I'll never even be able to approach. It slapped me back."

Silverman decided then and there to make Halliwell his project, to bring the nerdy kid out of his shell. He talked Halliwell up to his friends, praising his intellect and his writing. He introduced the boy around, lending him some of Silverman's social cache'. He encouraged him to publish his works, or at least to read them at some of the college's open mike nites for poetry and prose.

It was at one of these events that Bill Halliwell met Elizabeth Alcate, and the rest, as they say, is history.

Elizabeth--Bess as only he would call her--was a madwoman. She was wild, cadaverously pale, beautiful, promiscuous, talented, brilliant, a flame that one could only look at for so long before getting burned, and she had burned quite a few. Bill Halliwell would have considered her so far out of his league he'd never have tried, but first time she heard Halliwell read at an open mike, she had decided he was worthwhile, had chatted him up, and had dragged him into her bed for a long, exhausting, and occasionally athletic weekend, punctuated by intense conversation.

In the course of those discussions, she made two things clear: first, that she intended to continue sleeping with him and second--and more painfully--that he was far from the only one she was going to continue sleeping with.

Thus began the tempestuous, decades long relationship between the two of them. She became his joy and his sorrow, acting as unfailing editor and promoter for his writing and lavishing praise and adulation and sex on him for every success, only to turn and break his heart by going off with other men--and sometimes other women-- often right in front of him. For her part--though she'd never admit it to his face--she only felt herself when next to his calm kindness, only to have him push her away when she crossed some emotional line she'd failed to track.

It became the pattern for their lives together, coming together, breaking apart, drifting back together again like powerful magnets floating in rough waters.

He learned early on that every success, every achievement, brought her closer to him, so he applied himself to both his schooling and his writing. He turned his class work around, and produced volumes of poetry and prose, with Bess and Silverman standing by like proud parents whenever he'd do a reading.

His first great success was a failure. Finally convinced by Bess to submit some of his work for publication, he started at the top, sending a science fiction story to **Analog** magazine, then the top of the pyramid for short fiction in that genre. The rejection letter he received would have crushed him, but it came from John Campbell himself, **Analog**'s legendary editor, and read, in part "though this does not meet our current needs, I'd like to encourage you to submit to us again. I rather like your style of writing." It was all he needed. Halliwell threw himself into writing, missing with his next submission, but then scoring with the next three.

By the end of three years, he'd published countless poems, six short stories, a novella, completed a masters in computer technology, and Bess had moved in with him.

The next few years were ones of relative success for the three of them, Bess and Halliwell and Silverman. The Air Force pissed Silverman off for some reason he rapidly forgot about, and he wound up going into naval aviation, attending flight school at Pensacola, getting his wings, and serving as a fighter pilot in both gulf wars, and ultimately as wing commander. Bill Halliwell continued to write with moderate success, including one mediocrely successful filmscript, and taught and wrote on emerging computer technologies.

When Halliwell's mother became ill, he bought a small house in central Florida to get her away from Maryland's admittedly mild winters and moved her and Bess south. He taught at New College, wrote his stories, and went off for doses of praise and occasional seductions to science fiction conventions. Bess, for her part, became a thing in the real estate community, made unreasonable amounts of money, had numerous affairs, some of which she rubbed in Halliwell's face, endured occasional bouts of sickness from Lupus, and irritated the neighbors. Halliwell's mother gardened peacefully and enjoyed the sun.

Two events changed life for this bucholic and utterly American little commune. First, inevitably, Halliwell's mother died.

It was on a balmy summer night. Bess, who had gone from being a hopeless to really a quite acceptable cook, had made them dinner and was in an uncharacteristically uncombative mood. The conversation had, for once, been pleasant and free of tension. Sylvia, Halliwell's mother, had been in a fine mood as well, though she complained of being tired. As always, she had hugged him, kissed him on the forehead, and said "you're a wonderful son" like always. Then she had turned in. Sometime during the night, in her sleep, she slipped away. Bess had found him the next morning, sitting on the edge of his mother's bed, holding her cold hand, and smiling. "Not at all a bad end," he'd said, "not at all."

The second thing that happened was that his books were ripped off the shelves.

It was in the beginnings of the craziness in America, and the most recent group of loons to take over the State of Florida had declared a jihad on works fostering "immorality, wrong ideas, and great art that lies." A list of authors was banned statewide, and the new supreme court ultimately refused to hear the challenge, saying it was defending "community values." Halliwell was one of those slated for the ban.

At the initial hearing, Halliwell had argued calmly and patiently. "These are alternative worlds, alternative futures intended to teach a moral lesson by taking the curcumstance out of our present time and space." he'd said, "Those who read these--the community for whom it is intended, understand these distinctions, they 'get' the difference between the reality in my writing and their own." The words had, of course, fallen on deaf ears. The ban was part of "the agenda" and would not be questioned. "What if children saw these?" they said "what if foreigners read them and got the wrong idea about America?" "What Idea about America will foreigners get if America bans all writing the state doesn't like?" said Bill Halliwell, sealing his fate. The works were banned, his royalties seized for government coffers.

Bill fumed for three days. The Fleet was fairly young then, and already the subject of invective from the same folks that had banned his work. "Maybe I should move there." Bill Halliwell said. Bess surprised him. She wasn't enthusiastic about it, mind you, but "Maybe we should," she said, "I'm bored with this shit anyway."

And so they did.

Ever the pragmatic one, Bess had made the arrangements. She had put their accounts into offshore banks, had sold the house and shifted most of their furniture into storage. This was, of course, just to be for a while, just till things settle down and people come to their senses. She had gone with Bill to select a boat, something comfortable enough to stand for a while and small enough to handle. She had helped him refit it to Fleet specifications, sealing the thru hulls and installing composters and solar cells and building a rafting plank.

On a bright summer morning, they had driven down to the docks and climbed aboard, simply abandoning their car with the keys in the ignition. He had sailed with friends often enough as a boy, and it all came back to it easily. One pull on the sheets and they were gone.

Their acceptance in the Fleet was immediate and enthusiastic. There were enough sci-fi fanatics among the crew to know well who he was and all too well what had happened. Still, they took fleet names. Bill became Marcus, as in Marcus Brutus as in the role he would love to play to America's new "Caesar." Bess had become "Mab" but as happened all too often, it simply hadn't stuck. She was Bess until she died.

Truth to tell, "Marcus" was bored with writing. He was out of ideas, out of patience, and frankly ready for a new challenge. He had volunteered to help with the Fleet's computer system and at the end of his first year with the fleet, had approached Carlin with his idea for the ansible.

The fleet had been depending on what Carlin had called his "information ship", and old scow serving as cell phone node over which text messages, non radio voice, and internet communication moved. It worked....sort of...during rafting, but with the fleet under sail, it was easy to drop out of communication with the ship. Moreover, a single act by an outside power (read, the Americans) or a bad storm could strip the fleet of all its networking capability.

To Marcus, the problem was simplicity itself. He could create a distributed network that would operate without a center. The computers would talk to each other using short range, high frequency transfer, and they could use a custom operating system that would act as a firewall to the outside world. Viruses and trojan horses simply wouldn't work in them, and though they could transfer programs and games for other computers in the fleet, that tranfer couldn't infect the ansible network. The bandwith of the fleet would also be greatly increased.

 "It would be a combination computer, media center, cell phone, and internet connection" he'd said to Carlin" but with no center to the network, nothing that could be a target. We'd use our own design and our own software, so it would be almost impossible for anyone to crash the system from the outside." Carlin had been impressed. Marcus had tricked up the first three ansibles from surplus electronics kicking around in a Fleet storage ship, and after a little judicious debugging, they'd worked just fine. The office of the Quartermaster created a new post, the Signals officer, and had nominated Marcus to it.

Marcus rapidly made himself a fixture. He was calm, collected, invariably well researched, and a real asset in the often contentious meetings between the officers and Council. Moreover, as the ansibles prolifereated, the Crew began to realize just what a gem the system was. More and more uses were found, and contacts in America indicated that the Americans thought that the lack of cell traffic meant that the Fleet's cell system had failed and that the breakup of the floating nation must be immenent. Marcus had just laughed. When the Quartermaster requested retirement, Marcus was the logical choice. He assumed the office with a deceptive ease and grace. After only a few years with the fleet, he was firmly one of the leaders, and he was loving it.

Bess, for her part, also found work within the Quartermaster's office. Irritating as she could be, she was an ace investor, and soon found herself coordinating the Fleet's investments abroad.

When Carlin died so suddenly, the Council was thrown into disarray. This was the first real crisis under Carlin's new Articles, and replacing a figure as commanding and pivotal as Carlin was an instant problem. The Council dithered. The Crew brought foward suggestion after suggestion. Some demanded a plebicite. After two interminable days of arguement, Marcus brought forward two suggestions. The first was that the Council use the opportunity to clean up the line of command, shuffling around some of the new offices that had been created of the last few years so that they were logically under the officers they should be under, placing like with like. The second was that they stick to Carlin's original insipiration of the Admiral as city manager and not worry so much about it. "Just put someone in who can do the day to day of the job." he said "let greatness worry about itself." Then he went home to dinner with Bess.

The next day, he learned that the Council had taken his suggestions, had stayed up all night, gotten--typically--very drunk, and had done a really very competent job of reorganizing the Officers of the Fleet. He was a little surprised to find his name removed as Quartermaster. He was more than a little surprised when he saw his name written in as Admiral.

He wasn't their first choice. Some thought he lacked the necessary panache. Others felt he was doing too well as Quartermaster to take him out of the post. Ultimately, though, his steadiness and intelligence prevailed, that and the fact that--being well liked among the crew, and well respected as well--they knew he would be accepted. They had no idea how well they'd chosen.

When he told Bess, she'd laughed so hard she'd nearly pissed herself.

23. Cat of Ganymeade

Responsibility comes easily in the Fleet. Those that can, do, and are expected to.

Cat's father had once told her, "one of the great weaknesses of bureaucracies is that not only doesn't anyone want to take responsibility for what they do, they don't want to give *you* responsibility either, for fear *they'll* be blamed for what you do. It all becomes this kind of numbing paralysis where every time a challenge comes up, the first reaction isn't to deal with it, it's to find out who to *blame* for it."

The Fleet had none of those problems. If anything, responsibility was too easy to come by. There was a kind of frontier ethos here, in which anyone willing and with a modicum of qualifications to tackle a job usually got to do it. That was the story for Cat and Natasha in spades.

Natasha had been off on a shopping trip when she'd helped one of the Fleet's kids classes wrangle an unruly blue crab back into its aquarium. The following day she'd run into them again, laughing and joking with the kids. By the third encounter, Bev, who ran the little school pod, had convinced her to volunteer. The kids loved her. She was beautiful and funny and soft spoken and treated them like adults. Just her presence seemed to calm and focus them. "My niche" she said to Bev, "I think." Bev had to agree.

Cat's story was a little more extreme. After her impromptu marksmanship demonstration, Hank had convinced her to join the Constabulary and had raced her through the basic weapons training, which she did with ease. In only a few weeks, he had turned basic marksmanship classes over to her. "These new kids shoot like they're in some movie." he said, "the only safe place to stand when they're shooting is directly in front of the target. Whip them into shape." Surprisingly, she found she could.

She learned in due course the Constabulary's procedures, how to operate the equipment, including the handful of Fleet weapons--crude, clever, and robust devices that were probably more effective than anyone outside dreamed--and how to deal with crisis situations. With her sailing skills, she was soon assigned to Patrol, serving as gunner on a Vesper in the mornings, teaching in the afternoons.

After only nine months of this, she was given her own boat. "We're shorthanded," Hank had said. Privately, he had seen that she was one of his best. She had proven herself smart and level headed and Hank had come to trust her even over some of his more experienced officers. The boat she was assigned was the **Grendle**, one of the oldest of the Vesper fleet, cobbled together quickly but solidly in the early days of the Carlin Admiralty, she sported what was often referred to as a 'workboat' finish. Rough as she appeared, she sailed beautifully, and her transparent crabclaw sails could drive her through the water at surprising speed. Carlin had realized that what most patrol boats did was. . .well. . .patrol, and the sails had given the little boats surprising range. Like the other Vespers, her engines were a biodiesel/electric hybrid, running on seaweed oil, that could push the little boat to a 28 knot plane. An old 20mm protruded from her bow hatch, functional--barely--and battered, but the Carlin Projector amidships was new, as was its stock of missles.

The fact that Cat was younger than the other three members of her crew didn't seem to bother them. She had already served as firearms instructor for two of them, and that qualified her as an authority figure, she guessed. Regardless, they all called her "skipper," took orders with grace (albeit with honesty if they disagreed), and worked as a team.

So her days were spent aiding vessels in distress, running supplies to other patrol ships, herding ships back into Fleet formation on sails, assisting with the raftngs, and doing 'chickenhawk runs' facing down mammoth American frigates when they tested how close they could get to the fleet.

At the end of patrol, she would ansible Natasha, who was usually home by then, hit the markets, and maybe a wine shop, and head home to the little **Ganymeade** and her partner. She remembered one Wednesday when the patrol had been exhausting. There had been a chilly, wet mist all day, and they'd spent most of the patrol trying to upright a flipped sailboat full of British tourists that had set out from Abaco in far to heavy air and had gotten the sheets snarled. By the time she got back to the raft, the sun had set, everything was slick with salt spray, and she was chilled to the bone. She'd ansibled Natasha for a grocery list, but they only needed wine. Still, she'd managed to fall on her ass getting back up the gangway from the wine shop and had hit the rail of the little weekender in a foul mood.

But inside, the tiny cabin was warm and dry and lit by the glow of an oil lamp, and--despite a long day of her own with the school-- Nat had made a stew which filled the cabin with scents of rosemary and garlic. There was fresh bread from the Svenson's Bakery Boat, and Jamaican goat cheese with beignets for dessert. Nat had gotten her out of her wet things and the two of them had cuddled up under a blanket against the chill, eating and drinking wine and watching some old movie on the little ansible screen together. Abruptly, Natasha burst out laughing.

"What?!" said Cat, startled.

"So," said Nat, grinning at her, "this is married life." and nuzzled closer.

The two of them were asleep in each others arms before the credits rolled. After that evening, Nat always referred to herself as being Cat's "wife." Cat found she didn't mind at all.

Cat knew she had come full circle when the **Grendle** intercepted a little O'day 20 on its way into Fleet space. The boat was crewed by a teenage couple. The girl looked pregnant. The boy, probably all of seventeen, mostly looked terrified.

She brought the **Grendle** alongside, forgetting how quiet the vessel could be. The kids didn't know they were there until she was less than two feet off their starboard side. It terrified them all the more. Still, Cat was cautious. The Americans had pulled this kind of shit before.

"Afternoon," she said, noting that they couldn't take their eyes off the guns leveled at them to look directly at her. "You're a ways from shore. Do you need navigational assistance to get back home? Happy to oblige."

The boy finally got his center back and looked up at her.

"We're not going home m'am." he said. Mam? "We came to join the fleet."

Cat looked at them a moment, remembering when she had been in that place.

"Heave to and prepare to be boarded."

They did the inspection by the numbers, like always. Cat was unimpressed by their boat maintenance skills--but then, who knows how they'd gotten the thing--but their radio and some of their other gear had been cleverly disguised as cereal boxes or canned goods, and they had docking planks, she noticed, crude, but up to spec.

"You've been planning this a while."

"Yes ma'm." they nodded.

"It's 'yes, skipper'. Set your heading for 170. That will take you to the raft. Another boat will meet you there and take you into dock. Heading anywhere else would be a bad idea, you understand?" they nodded "You've got a CB in there. We monitor 6. If you get in trouble or get lost, give a shout and we'll help you. Making any other transmissions would also be a bad idea, you read me?"

"Yes m....yes skipper."

She smiled. "Good." and swung herself with practiced ease back onto the Vesper. "Good luck." she said. God, had she looked that young? "And welcome." She slid back into the cockpit and thumbed a quick message to the Constabulary that the kids were coming. Her crew all had the same smiles. They had all been there once. They all remembered.

So it was that Cat and Natasha came to their second Mayday gathering as full members of the Fleet, full as solid citizens of their community. Back home they had been children, as most Americans were eternally held children, their every move and thought noted and controlled and judged. Here, their destiny was in their own hands. The choice, risky as it had seemed, had been so unbelievably right.

It was Mayday, the Agoura had been set. The names of each of the crew, scrimshawed into bone, rested in the racks, and over the last day most of the crewmembers had made at least the pretense of inspecting the names, making sure their own was there, making sure none of the deceased or outcast remained. As Constabulary, Cat was in full 17th century drag, headset disguised beneath her long hair, cutlass at her side, fleet carbine with a hailshot charge under it's

barrel slung across her shoulder jungle style. She
looked at the other Constables, guarding the Agoura
before the ceremony. Bristling with blades and guns,
period leather snapsacks concealing gas masks and
grenades. . . .they looked fierce. She realized she knew
just how fierce. She had taught many of them basic gun
handling, and had been with them for over a year of
snapfire classes and sabre classes and martial arts
classes and simulations and small squad tactics
sessions. Fleet training was continuous, unending, and it
had made the Constabulary the equal of any marine
troops in the world. She felt proud.

Over by one of the pavilion posts, keeping out of the
sun, Natasha was beaming at her. Pure, unabashed
adoration.   Cat sometimes couldn't believe how lucky
she was.

A Boatswain's pipe sounded. The Council and Officers
filed in, followed by a mass of Crewmembers and their
families. The naming ceremony had begun. Cat fell back
next to Natasha. The moment the officers took their
seats, she was off duty, passing her responsibilities on
to the Constables that came in with Hank and the
Officers. Now she could relax, just another crewman,
and enjoy the show.

The Councilman of the First Seat pulled the strap, and
the bone tiles with the names of the crew cascaded
from their rack into a huge, blown glass bowl.
Everything transparent, everything in the open was the
rule. A precocious young girl of about 6, naked save for
the flowers braided in her corn rowed hair, began picking
out the tiles, one for each of the 12 Council seats.
They began with the 12th, the Marine Affairs seat, and

ended with the first seat, the Chair of the council. Each Councilman would read the name handed them and then take their place in the crowd. Their Vice Council would then step into their seat, and the crewman called, the new Vice Council, would take the seat behind them if they were present. Failing that, someone delegated by them or by the Admiralty would stand in, just till the ceremony was over, filling their place in this, the planet's most representative government.

The tike pulled a tile, and the tile was passed to the 12th Council seat, who stood and solemnly intoned "Stephen of the **Tortuga**.", then set the tile in the rack of Councilmen, removed his own, and joined the crowd. The older woman who had been his Vice Council took his seat, and so they progressed.

"YARRRR!" growled the crowd, in mock Pyratical enthusiasm.

"Would they get you to stand in, " asked Natasha, "if someone wasn't here?"

"Maybe. . ." said Cat ". . .probably. They'll usually call Constabulary to stand in since they know we're here."

Stephen of the **Tortuga**, a tough looking old coot in his seventies, took his place as 12th seat Vice Council, nodding gracefully to his friends.

"Good choice for that one, " said Natasha, "Old Steven designed the Tortuga boats. He'll be good in Marine Affairs."

"How'd you know that?" said Cat.

Natasha grinned. "Just did a unit on them with the kids...."

"Eleventh Seat, Starr of the **Cybele**"

"YARRR!" said the crowd. Cat looked around, grinning to herself. Bottles were being freely passed. Pipes were being lit and passed. Spacy Starr, wrapped in her eternal tie dyes, took her place in the line and the old Eleventh Seat joined the party.

"Tenth Seat, Ash of the **Lancer**."

"YARRR!"

"Ninth Seat, Fish of the **Fish**"

"YARRRRR!!!" said the crowd.

"Eighth Seat, Lysander of the **Spartan**"

"YARRRRR!" said the crowd, getting louder with each one. Lysander hadn't made it. Probably fifty people had just ansibled him. They made one of the Constables, Rob of the **Pelleanor**, stand in.

"Seventh Seat, Cyndi of the **Maitland**"

The YAARRR was huge this time, followed by shouts and applause. Cyndi had, as an infant, pulled the very first of the tiles for the council seats.

"Sixth Seat, Alex of the **Camel**"

No Alex. Hank motioned for Stacy, one of the

other Constables, to stand in.

"Fifth Seat, Leo of **Leo's Big Ugly Boat**"

The YARR was tempered by laughter. Leo barely made it up to the chair. Leo was very very drunk.

"Fourth Seat, Beatrix of the **Cannibis**"

SERIOUS YAAR. Beatrix grew pot that was fully capable of crawling to your boat under its own power.

"Third Seat, Cassis of the **Oargasm**"

Another no show. Hank looked her way, but Larry of the **Nam Singh** leaned over to ask him something, and got himself elected as stand in.

"Second Seat, Carlos of the **Mariel**"

"YAAAAARRRRR" Everybody loved Carlos.

And Cat looked at these people, her crewmembers, her friends. Ever so often, generally unexpected, always unbidden, there is a moment which defines you, which changes you. It's that flash that rewires your reality, and leaves you breathless and buzzing, and forever unable to go back to the way you were before, even to remember how it felt before. That was this moment, right after the calling of the Second Seat, and the way she would always remember it. She looked at the crew, young and old, in pirate drag and boat drag and naked and glistening with water. She looked at the children, jumping up and down with excitement. She looked at the adults, half drunk, laughing with joy, absolutely glowing, absolutely in love with their lives and their freedom and each other. She looked at Nat, laughing so hard tears were rolling down her cheeks and shouting for Carlos and Cyndi and all the others. In that moment, something changed for Cat. She had been in the crew. In years to come, in that moment, right after calling of the Second Seat, she would say she had *become* crew, and was forever changed by it.

"First Seat, Cat of the **Ganymeade**"

Across the Agoura, Hank, uncharacteristically, began to giggle.

24. The Passing

It had been too good a day, which concerned him.

Marcus had spent the Wednesday the way he always did
when they rafted: Up just after dawn and a swim in the
warm waters of the Caribbean, a big breakfast at
Tooley's, morning meetings with the Bosun and
Quartermaster and their staffs which spilled over
through a light lunch into the afternoon. It had gone
alright, he guessed. Typically, anyway. The planning
meeting with the Constable and Master at Arms--their
now traditional what-do-we-do-if-the-Americans-go-
nuts-THIS-cycle meeting--had actually been pretty
productive. Marcus had been dreading the meeting with
the Councilors in the afternoon, especially since the
FIrst Seat, Clancy of the *Lucerne,* had been having
some kind of family problems lately and couldn't find his
ass with both hands. First Seat handled all the
scheduling, and that was a hassle he didn't need. But
the girl from *Ganymeade* that was Clancy's vice
Council--the one Hank seemed to be grooming--had
stepped up the task nicely and things had actually run
smoother than usual. So the day had wound itself away.
The sun was out, the waters calm, the breeze

freshening.

Meetings done he had spent an hour or so putting in some target practice to blow off steam, and then off to *Asklepius* to see Bess. Afternoons were usually her good times. She'd never done mornings.

Bess. . .

She had been bad lately, out of it for most of the month and all of this rafting, and Marcus knew, sadly, that it could only go one way. He had seen her every day this rafting, had tried to read to her as usual. He wasn't sure she even knew he was there, and the medical orderlies on *Asklepius* were uncharacteristically quiet around him. Quiet and gentle and sad, for all their attempts to be pleasant and cheerful with him. During a night of drinking, Hank had said to him "She's suffered so long, Marcus, maybe it would be a blessing" and he'd muttered some kind of assent. . .

. . .but what on earth would he do without her?

But today, today she was amazingly focused and chatty, her eyes luminous. She seemed almost desperate to chat with him, catching up about people, about weather, about anything. She told him she loved him, which she seldom did. "I have been so proud of you, " she said, brightly, " so proud to be with you these last few years, have I told you that?" He'd chatted with her, and held her hand and kissed her, and they'd talked about what they might do for fun when she got better. He'd brought her a new book to read to her.

But after only a few minutes of listening to him read, she'd fallen into an alarmingly deep sleep, snoring softly.

He looked at her a long while.

"She seems much better today" the orderly said
cheerfully. "She wasn't that lively this morning."
Marcus had just smiled and said to call if they needed
him.

He knew what was coming. He'd remembered his mother
before she died doing this same odd surfacing, as if
they were desperate to touch base one last time before
they passed.

Still, he felt oddly at peace. He'd stopped back at
Tolley's, really just for a beer, but had wound up getting
a really magnificent flounder dinner, way more than he
needed to eat, but what the hell. The stars were out by
the time he got back aboard *Dragonfly*. He didn't
bother to turn in. He poured himself a brandy and began
reading the book he brought for Bess. Years later, he
always wondered why he never could remember the title.

The call came a little after 2AM, just about the time he
thought it would. "It was very peaceful." they said "do
you want to see her?"

No. Not like that.

He'd made a few calls--Hank and Rosie and a few others-
-and then settled in with the rest of the novel to wait
for dawn. The word would get out fast, but Bess had
been adamant about her final plans.

Just before the sun rose, Admiral Marcus, his
Constable, his Bosun, and a handful of others were on
the deck of *Asklepius*. Just as the sun broke the

horizon, the boat slipped its moorings and headed away from the raft toward the east and the sunrise. Very few of the Crew were awake to see it going. Those that did see it knew immediately what it meant.

He didn't want to see her, not dead. Sick, okay, sleeping, okay, even dying, but he didn't want to hold the image of her dead in his memory. They brought him the necklace she wore, the one he'd given her years ago since she'd never been willing to take a ring from him. He gave them the novel, the battered paperback he'd brought to read to her, to put in with her. They looked at him oddly. "We didn't get a chance to finish it." he'd said "she'd hate that."

Iron Bess was sewn in a white sailcloth sack with two lengths of heavy chain by her sides and a battered paperback on her breast. They laid her on a plank at the stern of the boat.

Everyone expected Marcus to say something, but the words wouldn't come. Nothing would. Just tears and this horrible clenched feeling in his throat. He laid his hand on her chest, half expecting to feel her breathing. All he felt was the canvas and the book beneath it. He managed to to choke out "bye, baby. . ." but after that no more words would form, only tears and loss.

He nodded to the orderlies who slipped her into the sea. He couldn't watch her go. It was the single most horrible moment of his life.

They all stood there, with no sound except the water and Rosie sniffling softly in the background. To the east, the sun rose hot and bright in a clear sky. A seagull came and lit on the stern of the boat, regarding them curiously.

"Well. . . ." said Marcus, finally. ". . .well. . ."

Then Marcus and the *Asklepius* turned back to the fleet, a fleet which seemed suddenly ever so much emptier.

25. Natasha

Nat was amazed at how fast things had happened, how easily she had grown into this new life. She even thought of herself as Natasha now. Natasha, the teacher. Natasha, who had become one of the go-to people for advice on childcare. Natasha, the entirely respectable wife of the first vice chair of Council. Natasha of **Ganymeade**, and happy with it.

Nat was amazed at how rapidly her old life had fallen away; school and parents and neighbors, it all seemed so impossibly distant. She had gone through a period of feeling badly about leaving them, about going without a word. She thought of emailing them, or trying to mail or call, but knew for certain that such communications would be traced, with unknown results for her, Cat, and the Fleet. So she sat on her small sorrows and tried to revel in the happiness of at last being with Cat and being free.

Until Hank had introduced her to Roberta Veracruz. Roberta was a Venezuelan national. Roberta lived on Margarita Island, and occasionally had contact with the Fleet on it's yearly cycles.

Roberta didn't exist.

"Everyone that leaves has messages to send back." said Hank. "Everyone wants to know news from home, to let people know they're okay, just to touch base somehow." In response, he went on, the Fleet had created a number of imaginary correspondents, untraceable people in untraceable countries to write to the heavily censored and patrolled Net in the Americas. Fleet members trained in the deception would send messages, chatty letters consistent with a disinterested third party passing along and receiving information. Hank showed her how to put in the request.

So "Roberta" dutifully drafted a simple, grammatically awkward note to Nat's parents. She was just passing on a message. Nat was fine, married and happy, living in the inaccessible--to the American government, anyway-- interior of Venezuela. "Roberta" would pass along another message as soon as she could.

Nat was pleased.

So she curled up inside her life with Cat. In America, she had felt out of control of her life, constantly on the precipice, at risk and off balance. Here she felt warm and safe and happy.

Working with the kids had caught her by surprise. She had never really been around children, not as an adult, and had no way of knowing she would love it so. She loved teaching and playing with them, loved comforting them and understanding them. Most of all she loved watching the lights kick on, as those, hot, bright intelligences suddenly registered and deciphered one secret of human life after another.

Bev, the woman who had founded and ran the school pod, told her: "there are a number of gifts of pedagogy: patience, kindness, calm, unflappability, knowledge, and grace." she'd ticked them off on her fingers like counting children, "you have all of them, Nat. " she'd said, "you were born to this."

And Natasha loved it; Loved swimming naked with the kids, squirmy and slippery as eels, loved singing songs with them, laughing with them, crying with them. . . .she loved every moment of it.

How would she tell Cat that she wanted one of her own?

26. Rising Waters

Jim Silverman leaned back in his seat in the little center salon of **Dragonfly** and regarded his host. Marcus, the man he knew as Bill Halliwell, was tanned, muscular, greying, and healthy. In fact, Silverman was struck with how healthy all of the Fleet citizens looked. A life on the sea seemed to suit them. He was also amazed at the authority that the once shy and gangly Halliwell projected. A smooth confidence he'd often seen in those who had successfully shouldered responsibility. Overwhelmingly, though, what struck him was the sadness in Admiral Marcus, the marks of loss that no amount of health, competence, or authority could mask.

"I'm sorry about Bess." he said finally, "I'm sorry I missed her."

Marcus smiled and refilled his bourbon. "I know. It's okay. She asked after you often. I think she missed the times the four of us spent in Florida."

"I miss them too, " said Silverman, "and Maggie. . .and my wasted youth....and my wasted middle age."

"Here's to wasting our old age as well." said Marcus, toasting him. "In retrospect, I don't see how it could have been any different. . . at least, any better. So here we sit, two old widowers, both admirals, both drinking bourbon. Whouda thought."

"Yeah." said Silverman, fingering the edge of his glass. He didn't want to launch into this, not right away, but his time was limited. Ah well. "Bill, this next year is going to be a fucking nightmare for both of us. . ."

"Your bosses planning on hitting us again?"

Silverman laughed. "My bosses! My bosses have been planning on hitting you again for the last ten years. Everybody in the Pentagon keeps telling them why they can't or shouldn't. We just keep delaying them. . . .that's not it."

Marcus pulled himself up to the table. He looked at Silverman, slumped in the **Dragonfly**'s little settee. Marcus thought he looked exhausted, sallow. He could do with a good long sail, he thought, with a good drinking binge, or maybe getting laid. . . .of course, so could I.

"What's up, Jim?" said Marcus "I know you liked Bess, but you didn't swing this trip just to see her off, or just to see me."

Silverman took a deep breath, let it out all at once, clearing his head from the bourbon. He fished in his briefcase and dropped a bulging file in front of Marcus. "You're right." he said simply.

Marcus thumbed through the file. It was full of tide schedules, temperature charts, and depth soundings.

Strangely for a military report, there was no index, no summary, no precis, no tidy way to make sense of it. Just reams of research and conclusions.

"Can you give me a summary, Jim?"

"I can and I will," said Silverman, "but I still want you to read it while I'm here. I need for you to understand this, every bit of it."

"Okay. " said Marcus, "what am I looking at? This isn't an official release."

"You're right,"said Silverman, "it isn't. This is the report from my climatologist, and we deliberately made it hard to casually comprehend. The summary is pretty simple. That first section, the blue sheets, are about the Greenland ice sheet. Bill, it's about to go. It could be going as we speak, and a significant amount of that ice will wind up in the north Atlantic over the course of only a few weeks."

"How much of a sea level rise we looking at? My people tell me about 15cm."

"That's about right. Capt. Kelly estimates between 9 and 14."

"But we've known that." said Marcus. "That's handleable. . ."

"The problem is, no one asked what 15cm will do to the REST of the ice sheets."

"Ah." Said Marcus. "gotcha. . . ."

"The Antarctic, particularly, is vulnerable. Kelly estimates that it could go within a month of Greenland. Add that, and we're looking at four meters. Maybe five. . ."

"Bad."Marcus started to say." I was thinking...."

But Silverman cut him off. "I'm not done yet."

"Okay." said Marcus, settling back in his chair.

"Ever hear of an island called La Palma?" said Vice Admiral Silverman.

Marcus was very quiet for a time, then said, simply. "Leave me with this for a bit. You must be starving. Taffy's, the cafeboat just down the dock, serves some great food. They all know you're my guest. Just go have what you want. I'll come down when I'm done."

Silverman stepped out onto the gently undulating docking planks. The sun had just set, the sky was clear, and some of the stars were out. . .planets, really. It really is a beautiful place, he said to himself, though watching the scenery go up and down in waves would take some getting used to. It also had taken him a bit to get used to all the public nudity, but he decided, that he could live with it. Of course, being passed on the gangway by two beautiful naked young women didn't hurt.

He *had* been alone for too long.

Silverman made his way to Taffy's, a convivial little diner on an old shrimper that had been converted to sail.

Everybody knew who he was. Migod, he thought, how does Bill ever keep a secret in this place? He ordered dinner. The wine was good, the food was astonishing. He wished he could've enjoyed it more.

Back aboard **Dragonfly**, Admiral Marcus settled in with his bourbon and his reading. A decade ago, he'd not have been able to make heads or tails of this oceanographic jargon, but he'd been living and breathing this stuff for years now. This Kelly guy, he thought, knows his stuff. Captain Kelly was a scientist, and a sound one. He laid out the facts and his arguments in a clear, logical, and unemotional fashion. It didn't change the nightmare of the outcome.

The papers told the story of a tragic cascade of events that were unfolding as he was reading, probably unstoppable, unbelievably destructive. The minor failure in the Greenland ice sheet would cause a minor rise in sea levels, but that rise would lead to a sudden and dramatic destabilization of the already degraded Western Antarctic sheet. Most of the ice from the Ellsworth Mountains to the coast would find itself in a sudden migration waterward. The resulting sea level rise, taking place as quickly as over a few weeks, could be in the 4-5 meter range. . .

That wasn't the worst of it.

La Palma. It was a disaster waiting to happen that had been watched for nearly fifty years now. La Palma was an island in the Canaries. Half the island was an active volcano, the other half an extinct one. Decades ago, during a rather minor earthquake, nearly half of the southern part of the island had broken away and shifted several meters downslope. Studies concluded that basalt dikes within the dead volcano were retaining water, and that that water was acting as lubricant, allowing the mountain to slip.

A 5 meter rise would overtop the lower dikes, flashing to superheated steam on the hot rock, and that would cause the underpinnings of the mountain's face to give way.

The resulting splash--millions and millions of tons of rock falling into the sea all at once--would create a cavitation wave, a mega-tsunami, a wall of water over 600 meters high that would race across the Atlantic at some three hundred knots. The inundation would clobber the already flooded coast, driving the waters hundreds of miles inland. The wave could also cause even more ice to enter the ocean, raising the levels still further.

Nightmare.

Kelley's work was a thing of beauty. It left few loose ends, little room for argument. This was something unfolding right now. It was real, not potential. The disaster could be happening right now, the wave on its way as he sat there reading, and the fucking loons in Washington and Beijing who had blocked all discussion of global warming had only themselves to blame.

Silverman was just finishing his dessert when Marcus slid into the booth with him. The waiter had chips and salsa and a glass of Sangiovese in front of him almost before he sat down: the privilege of being a regular...and the Admiral.

"Well?" said Silverman.

"Well indeed. . ." said Marcus. He found he was hungry. "Thank you for this." he said, dropping the folder in front of Silverman and woofing down a handful of chips. "I'm not sure why you brought it though."

"How's that?" said Silverman.

"Don't get me wrong, we'll use the warning, and I thank you for it. Saved our bacon, and I appreciate it. But, Jim, you could've done that with an email. You've got more on your mind."

Silverman grinned at him. "It's hard for me to remember sometimes that you're not a clueless as you used to be."

Marcus grinned back at him. "Still feel that way most of the time."

"You're not. "said Silverman. "Look, if I send this to D. C., they'll pretend to ignore it, they'll 'take it under advisement' and I'll hear nothing else from it. What will happen is, quietly, they'll move the families of the Party's leaders out of harm's way, then begin to have meetings about how they can turn this to their advantage. The millions of dead won't bother them a bit."

"And?"

Vice-Admiral Silverman put the files back in Marcus' hands. "I want you to release this, Bill. Release it as if it were your own research. That way the islands will listen and the South Americans will listen and probably the EU will listen, and then maybe public opinion will get that gibbering monkey in the White House to listen."

"You know we'll have to check it out ourselves." said Marcus.

"I know. I hope you can prove me wrong."

"Isn't anybody else on this?" said Marcus.

"Not that we've noticed. Iceland may be, but they don't talk to anyone these days. The EU knows about the Western Sheet in Antarctica and about Greenland, but they don't seem to have put them together. Captain Kelly's got a way with this stuff. Half the time I can't make heads or tails of it in raw data form. He sees the patterns."

". . .and explains them pretty well." Marcus agreed.

"Bill, when this hits, even if there *is* warning, its gonna be hell on earth for the whole eastern seaboard of the Americas. It'll displace millions, and permanently, and I doubt if the farmers and cities inland are going to be exactly welcoming of all those mouths to feed. You folks have been living *on* the water for decades. Nobody has your kind of experience. If those people have a whisp of a chance for a life, it'll be a life like yours. But first, you have to survive it with your people and I have to keep Washington from bombing you into oblivion in the meanwhile."

The waiters at Taffy's stayed open late that night, accommodating two old friends who seemed to be chatting away long into the evening. They all knew the

Admiral, knew of his recent loss, respected and loved him. They didn't mind staying open. They thought the company would do him good.

Silverman slept late the next morning, rocked by the Hostel ship **Greenwich** through a deep and dreamless sleep. He woke to his flight out, to a dawn that was blood red over a pewter sea.

"Red sky at morning," he thought, "it figures. . ."

27. Cat

Responsibility come quickly in the fleet. Cat had gone from shooting instructor to patrol skipper, and now was vice-Council to the important first seat of the government. At 20, it was heady, and seemed rather unreal, but then, she realized, no one in the Fleet *knew* your age, or your background, or what you had come through to get here. It was a clean slate, and one that, if you had the will, you could make real use of.

Clancy of the **Lucerne**, the first seat council, was a kind and intelligent man in his forties. Showing remarkable foresight, he had drafted a whole series of instructions prior to stepping into the first seat role for whomever would be his new vice-council. It had been a huge relief for Cat. The first Chair was the Chairperson of the Council, setting the agenda, acting as parliamentarian, and in general acting as the pivot on which the machine of the Council system rotated. It was a position of great responsibility, and Clancy's careful notes helped her slide into it with a degree of ease and confidence. She didn't realize at first that Clancy of the **Lucerne** had his own agenda.

Clancy's story had been typical of the fleet. He and his wife Kathy had been well educated, cultured, well-liked, and utterly homosexual. Their marriage was a cover for their true lives, and a way to have the family they'd both wanted. It had worked beautifully. So they'd become pillars of the community, spent long weekends partying with their 'single' friends Edward and Lindy, and, one sparkling summer afternoon, Kathy had given birth to their lovely little daughter Aerial. They were ecstatic.

But Kathy had had a difficult time with the birth, and hovered perilously close to renal failure. As a poor school teacher, and with her unable to work, Clancy hadn't been able to afford the medical care they both knew she needed. For two years, her health was touch and go, then it stumbled, collapsed, and failed. Clancy was a widower with a small child and a big secret. Lindy, Kathy's partner, had gone off the deep end. Edward had had to step in as surrogate parent, and rumors had brought the attention of the authorities. Hearings were scheduled. Lives were investigated. Edward and Clancy agreed, rather than lose Aerial to some state religious institution, that the fleet was the only answer.

But at dockside, Edward had gotten cold feet, had apologized profusely, and had simply driven away, leaving Clancy shattered, in tears, and with only two choices: lose his daughter forever, or sail away. He had cast off the mooring lines of the graceful **Lucerne**, swallowed his heart, and never looked back.

A teacher and painter, Clancy had soon become a fixture in the Fleet. Everyone knew him and Aerial, and though--badly burned at the heart level--he kept to himself, he was thought of as friend by a host of the crew, and his daughter as a delightful ornamentation for the docks on a summers day.

But now lovely Aerial, a precocious six year old, was fighting for her life with a congenital heart defect that had surfaced suddenly and was absorbing more and more of Clancy's attention. She had been back and forth to hospitals in Cuba for most of the previous year. It was only after three months as Vice-Council that he had come to Cat and had stunned her by announcing that he felt he had to step down.

Cat would have gone into high panic mode, but the Fleet had dealt with this before. Clancy had explained it simply: Cat would step into first Chair, but a new Vice-Council would be appointed, one who had formerly held the first Chair seat as Council. The very next day an emergency Council was convened, Cat took her office, and she met her new Vice-Council and tutor. In this case, the Council had tapped Molly of the **Lost Innocence**, a crusty old broad with a wicked sense of humor, a wardrobe that seemed to have been attacked by a herd of moths, and an aroma of gin and hasheesh that went wherever she did. Cat liked her at once.

Molly had a rare talent. She had spent thirty years as a medieval art historian at Virginia Commonwealth--a job that forced her to LIVE by details-- before she had walked away from it and joined the fleet with her husband. She was the most organized person Cat had ever seen; teaching her how to structure her agendas, how to prioritize the schedule, and how to do all of that effortlessly. On the day before Cat was to chair her first meeting, she had asked Molly "what do I do?" Molly had just laughed. "Do what you did when you first skippered for the Patrol, girl: Take command."

And so she had.

By the time of the next Mayday, the Council was running
smoothly and Cat had gained the respect of the Fleet.
By the articles, Cat would remain in first Chair,
completing her two years of service, but Molly would
step down in favor of a new, neophyte Vice Council.
When Tree of the **Wet Forest** had taken his place on
the bench behind her, she had handed him a sheaf of
papers, Clancy's notes and her own. "Read these" she
said simply, "you'll need them."

It was this Cat of **Ganymeade** that had taken her place
during a southward sail in a climactic meeting aboard
the luxurious **Maitland**. All the officers were there, and
old Stephen of **Tortuga**, the 11th seat, chair of
Maritime....and of course, Cyndi....it was her boat now.
The rest of the Council was listening in, connected by a
secured ansible link on their various boats.

Marcus lost no time. He detailed the information in
Capt. Kelly's papers and the likely outcomes.

"And we've confirmed this?" asked Stephen.

"Navigation has spent the last month tearing this
apart." said Marcus, indicating the wad of papers in
front of him. "If anything, Capt. Kelly understated the
problem."

"Meaning?"

"Meaning the wave and sea level rise will likely trigger
further breakdown in the Antarctic and Greenland ice

sheets, as well as degradation of the Siberian sheet. We will see additional sea level rise, probably substantial."

"Define substantial." said old Stephen.

"Maybe as much as 40 meters. . . .maybe more."

There was utter silence for a few moments, save the soft slap of water against the hull and one low whistle from the officer corps.

"So," said Cat finally, "what do you suggest we do?"

Marcus sat down on **Maitland's** elegant settee. He had been running on the excitement of adrenaline and purpose for the last month. Now that the meeting was here, he felt exhausted. He took a sip of water and looked at the cabinfull of expectant faces watching him, wanting him to be sure, to be right.

"We've studied the '05 Tsunami, and the '11 one in Oregon. We think we have some idea of how this will go down. After the wave, there'll be a whole lot of small boats who have taken to deep water to avoid it. We'll need to pick those up because they'll likely be short of supplies and there'll be no where for them to go to port. If the other waves are any indication, there will also be a whole lot of vessels in varying stages of damage washed out to sea, and we can use those to house survivors." If they listened any harder, thought Marcus, they'd be inside my head. "Hey I've never had this many people pay this much attention to ANYthing I've said before. . ."

"You've never had this much worth listening to before. " said old Stephen, grinning. The room erupted in laughter, the tension broken. Skillful, thought Cat. She wondered if they'd worked that out ahead of time.

Marcus continued, easier now. "We want to divide the fleet after next rafting. The bulk of the fleet will migrate across the Atlantic to just off the Namibian coast. We'll be safe from the main thrust of the wave there, and afterwards can cross to take care of Caribbean and South American survivors. A smaller fleet will head north to the Sargasso Sea, will ride out the wave there, and then will head into the east coast of America to help out. Once the wave has passed, we'll reunite the fleets and break a small fleet off for the Indian ocean to help with those trapped by ocean rise."

A voice from one of the Ansibles cut in jarringly: "Why is this our job, Marcus?" Later no one would remember which Council member had chimed in.

"I know this isn't our responsibility. I know we could just weather the wave and the rise in the waters and go on as we have, but what happens to the world happens to us, and ultimately we'll have to deal with it. We'll have to deal with refugees, with the lack of supplies, and with the changes in water level and quality. One of the reasons we were given this information is that some of the American Navy knows that we're the only ones with the experience and expertise to take on this job. I'd rather deal with it intentionally then panic when thirty thousand small boats come knocking at our door."

"The Americans have spent the last two decades beating the drum about how they're the last superpower, the greatest nation on earth, all the while carefully avoiding doing anything about the world's problems unless there was a profit in it. We've raked them over the coals for that, laughed at them, despised them for it. . . . Now I kind of feel it's time to put up or shut up."

Marcus looked around the cabin. He didn't need to ask. They were with him. The ansibles were silent.

Cyndi chimed in from up in the cockpit: "Marcus, you given any thought to governance? Communications could get iffy."

"Good call." said Marcus "and yes. We're suggesting that the existing first chairs take over the North Atlantic fleet and choose new temporary officers, the Vice Chairs will serve the southern fleet with the existing officer corps. That should give us an easy mix of experienced people who have worked together and new folks."

"Consensus?" said Cat, startling herself with how reflexive it was. There were mutterings of assent over the ansibles. No one objected.

"We'd also suggest that the first chairs choose a North Fleet Admiral from the existing Council." said Marcus, obviously please with how smooth this was going, " we suggest you, Stephen."

Every eye in the place looked at old Stephen of **Tortuga**, the old pirate who had been with the fleet from the first. Stephen grinned back at them, leaned back on his perch on one of the galley's counters, and simply said:

"No."

There was a momentary confusion.

"Look, "he continued "this could go on for years, even decades. This ain't gonna be just an unpleasant weekend folks. I'm 78 now. You need somebody that can give you some continuity no matter how long it takes."

Marcus waited for a moment for the buzz on the ansibles to quiet down. "Stephen, who would you recommend?"

Old Stephen gave a wicked little chuckle, obviously pleased with the attention.

"Her." he said, and pointed directly at Cat.

27. The Last Raft

The meeting went on into the night, and it was nearly
midnight before the exhausted crew made the difficult
night transits back aboard their own boats.
Ganymeade had been in tow behind the **Maitland** and
when Cat finally climbed aboard, she found Nat sleeping
naked in the cockpit. She was stunning, sleeping there
bathed in moonlight. Nat had always been beautiful, but
over the last few years in the fleet they had both taken
on muscle and tan. She could tell her about events
later. For now, Cat ran her fingertips across the soft
curve of her love's belly, eliciting a sleepy smile.
Natasha reached up and pulled Cat's mouth to hers.
Cyndi wouldn't mind towing them for a bit longer. For
now it would be lovemaking with the only one who had
ever held her heart, there in the open beneath a canopy
of moon and stars.

Tomorrow, the world would change forever.

The morning dawned warm and clear, with a sky full of
birds and an ansible full of messages, most
congratulatory or offers of help. Cat was surprised,
and a little taken aback. Even the public boards had few

objections to her as the Admiral of the little Northern Fleet. Perhaps she really had proven herself.

The command came to raft at midmorning, and by prior arrangement, Cat and Natasha's little **Ganymeade** tied up between the Marcus' **Dragonfly** and the **Maitland**. This would be the longest rafting ever, nearly a month, if the weather cooperated, and at the end of it the fleet would divide. There was a sense of the moment, of its weight, throughout the Fleet. The minute the docking planks dropped into place, the work began in earnest.

And there was so much work to do.

First, Cat had to assemble enough of a fleet to make life bearable while they waited for disaster. She put together a catalogue of needs, contacted those who volunteered, and then sought out others. They would need food stores, water, restaurants, pubs. . .they would need media and clothing and dentists and mechanics. . .they would need to be a fleet. Cat barely knew where to begin. She made lists. She made lists of lists. She made notes and scribbles and pages and pages of drawings that a day later even SHE couldn't decipher. "Let us help you, baby." Natasha kept saying, but she didn't know "Help with WHAT?" There were many, many offers of assistance, but she knew from her work in command that before she said yes, she'd damn well better have something for them to do, or they'd lose interest and drift away. The planning meeting was only at week's end. Cat began to feel the edges of panic. Putting her in charge had been a big step for the fleet, a grand gesture. If she met with Marcus and the others and fumbled it, if she let them down, their trust in her might never recover. But how to proceed? Two days passed, then three.

Sleep eluded her.

So it was that Cat came to be sitting in the lounge of the *ST. Croix*, a pub boat just acquired by the fleet, her table buried in legal pads and ram drives and charts and an untouched Red Stripe warming in front of her.

"How's it goin, skipper?" said a craggy voice. She looked up to see old Stephen standing next to the table with a pitcher of Margaritas in one hand and two glasses in the other.

"I have no earthly idea. . ." said Cat, shoving some papers aside to make room for the pitcher. Screw it. She needed a break.

"Quite a project," said Stephen, "see you're deep into it." He poured them both some of the white concoction into frozen glasses.

"Buried in it's more like it." said Cat "Trying not to get lost."

Stephen took a drink and chuckled "Y' sound like Bobby. 'member he usta talk like that early on. . ."

"Bobby?"

"Carlin. Admiral Carlin. 'member seein' him buried in papers like this. Hee. Brings it back." Stephen grinned at her. He was about something, but she knew better than to ask him directly. Stephen had his own way of going about things.

"You knew Carlin? I mean, in the early days. . ..that didn't come out right."

Old Stephen laughed and shook some of his grey mane away from his face. "Oooh yeah. I was working in Ocala, building boats for this big company. Big, goddam ugly fiberglass things, huge engines, just the sort of thing for some rich asshole to go around tearing up the scenery in. Bobby comes in with all these drawings, asking if we could do some fiberglass slipmolding for him. He'd been workin on this stuff for three years, had more facts and notes and drawings than you could imagine. Most of it on paper in those days too." he looked at her pile of legal pads, "See you're fond of paper."

"Need to handle it somehow." said Cat.

Stephen nodded. "So did Carlin. I've seen him fill the floor of a hotel room with paper, all laid out in ranks, and go stepping from one pile to the next as he talked. Anyway, his comin' by to ask about molding boat hulls led to him tellin me about the rest of this stuff, which let me ta tellin him about the boats I really wanted ta build, which hooked me into this project forever. Walked out of the factory the next day, found him and the folks around him, and never looked back."

"He must have been an amazing guy."

"To be honest, mam, he was a little nancy boy, faggoty enough to unnerve some people, and frankly pretty funny to watch when he got excited. . . .but he had a passion for this that was infectious, and he was smart as a whip. . " Stephen lowered his voice and leaned in toward her "but no smarter than you, lady. "

Something about the change in his voice took her aback. "Right now, mam, you're probably feeling a little buried in this, but I pointed you out ta them for a reason, spotted you the first day out with you and your girlfriend sailin' in here in that little boat of yourn. I've not been wrong about you a single day yet."

"Lets hope you aren't now." said Cat.

"Carlin started all this mess from dead scratch. You have all the fleet's resources. What he DID have that you lack was nearly seven years to think about it, to organize things, and to make his own stack of notes." He tapped her ansible. "The notes are in the archive, and believe me, the bastard took brilliant notes."

Old Stephen's eyes sparkled. Okay. THAT was what this was about.

"Perhaps I should check them out." Said Cat, now grinning at him. "Might make for some useful reference materials."

"Perhaps. . ." said old Stephen, grinning, back, ". . . you should."

She ordered them lunch and put her papers aside. The spent the early afternoon eating and drinking and talking of the early days, of Carlin and the fleet. Old Stephen was a poet of the water, and knew more about boats and the people who sailed them than anyone she'd met. They parted with him a bit hammered and Cat feeling weirdly confident.

That evening, with Natasha at a parent conference, Cat

bored into Carlin's notes in the archive. Old Stephen had been right. Carlin had detailed everything, notes upon notes upon notes, water consumption figures and food consumption figures, maintenance schedules, all of it laid out and cross referenced, all of it so orderly an eight year old could've navigated it. Having wandered lost in this stuff for days, it took her breath away. Carlin must have lived and breathed this stuff for a decade to produce a document like this. He must've had a mind like a mainframe. The files weren't stale either. He had used Marcus' publishing features in the ansible system to automatically update the information as new figures emerged. By the time Nat came home, the Admiral of the Northern Fleet knew what she had to do. Natasha stepped down from the cockpit with a bottle of wine and a chicken dinner and walked into an explosion of enthusiasm and facts and figures, followed by an explosion of passion--a release for Cat of all the pent up angst and frustrations of the last three days--that lasted well into the night.

That night, in a dream, she looked out of the porthole of the little *Ganymeade* to see her father, Old Stephen, and Bobby Carlin drinking and playing cards around an old crate on the dock. Her dad glanced over at her and smiled, then went back to his hand.

Things were going to be fine.

By the time the meeting rolled around in the salon of the *Maitland*, Cat was ready.

She used the plasma screen in the Maitland's luxurious lounge to project her charts. Between her own research and Carlin's, she had everything: times and tides and ship requirements, lists of supplies and sources, emergency supplies for after the wave hit and how they needed to be distributed. . . Stephen and Marcus just sat in the back with Nat and beamed like proud parents while she put on her show. Everyone else was stunned. It knocked their socks off. If anyone had had any doubts about Cat going into this, this laid them to rest. . . .for the moment at least. As she was leaving, Fleet Admiral Marcus stopped her at the dock and simply said "Impressive." Something in his voice ran a little thrill up her spine. All in all it was a great day. . .

Now all she had to do was assemble her fleet. She began making the rounds, firming up those who had volunteered, seeking out needed resources from those that hadn't or wouldn't. . .

Some came readily, excited by the adventure. Some came reluctantly, either through a sense of duty or because of some very careful arm twisting by Marcus or Old Stephen.

Some, of course, refused to leave the main fleet at all. But by the end of the week, she had the minimal fleet she needed. Others would join by the rafting's end, she knew, but there was no longer the desperation to find enough to make a working community.

That didn't end it of course. There were things Carlin couldn't have considered in his carefully laid out notes. There was the matter of the sargasso itself.

The Sargasso Sea is a slowly rotating region of the Atlantic east of Bermuda. Driven by the Gulf Stream, it is a calm lens of warm water cycling endlessly over the icy depths of the mid Atlantic, a thin garden over a vast icy desert. Food would be a problem. Winds like the reliable trades of the Caribbean did not exist there. Doldrums were the rule much of the year. Suppliers had to be found in Europe and Canada and the Bermudas to replace those in the tropical islands. Bermuda, particularly, would be their next door neighbors and had to be dealt with carefully, balanced as they were between the EU and the Americans.

So Cat dispatched her new Quartermaster, Amber of the *Evangelion*, a woman who could sweet talk you out of your spleen, to deal with Bermuda and their suppliers in the EU, and began working with some of the sea farmers with the fleet on developing food sources that would work within the warm, nutrient deprived waters of the Sargasso. Farming the Sargassum would take a major shift of gears from the fish cages they'd been used to, but the watermen convinced her it could be done.

Then there was the issue of the wave itself. Assuming they survived it as Marcus assured her they would, there would be hundreds, maybe thousands of refugees, probably low on supplies, possibly injured, cold, hungry, and terrified to deal with. There would be people in the water. There would be hundreds of derelict boats to recover and refit to house them. There would be debris and bodies and hazards to navigation, especially hundreds and hundreds of half-submerged steel shipping containers from the ports. And all of it, all of it, came down to Cat and her judgment. She found, to her great surprise, that she loved all of it.

Natasha had her own complex responsibilities. As one of the Fleet's teachers, and one who was definitely going with the Northern Fleet, it fell to her to organize schooling for their splinter of the greater Fleet. To find, cajole, and convince other teachers to join them, to try to figure out how many kids would be with them, and of what ages, to find facilities, materials, to try to come up with some kind of workable schedule for classes. . . .Natasha was in the thick of it. It was exhilarating.

Exhilarating or not, it was also exhausting.

At the end of what seemed the busiest week of her life, Cat found herself wandering down the docks at sunset, feeling like she'd been dropkicked down a flight of stairs. At least she was done for the day. Natasha would be at a parent teacher conference for at least several more hours. Those things could be worse than Patrol meetings, and a lot more contentious. Frankly, the fledgling admiral was happy just to have a few minutes of aimless down time.

So she took a glass of wine and walked down the long avenue of docking planks to watch the red sun settle over Mexico. Long streamers of orange clouds promised a fair coming day. Despite all the fatigue, she was wonderfully at peace. She stood there watching until the last scarlet began to fade from the Western clouds, then turned to head back to home, back to **Ganymeade** and Natasha.

At the opposite end of the dock, watching the stars rise in the East, sat a figure dangling his toes in the water.

Marcus.

Cat settled down beside him.

"You look as tired as I am." she said.

"Tired and wasted." he said, gesturing with the bourbon bottle he'd been drinking from. "Figured if we're taking tomorrow off, I'd indulge myself." He refilled her empty wine glass from the bottle. "You?"

"We've been pushing so hard, I'm kind of at loose ends." she said, and took a sip of the fire in her glass.

They talked for a long time, sharing the bottle and the stars. Cat of her life and Natasha and finding themselves in the Fleet. Marcus of his youth and Bess and her passing. All those things you so seldom get a chance to talk out. After a time, Cat was too buzzed even to listen. She just watched him talk. The startling similarities to her late father had long since faded into a real appreciation of Marcus; of his kindness and wisdom, of his generosity or spirit and his sadness. And then, almost inevitably, she was kissing him.

She awoke sometime after midnight aboard the **Dragonfly**. The moonlight through the open hatch pouring over empty glasses, discarded clothes, and condom wrappers, the hulk of the sleeping Marcus naked next to her in the moonlight.

Ohmigod, she thought, Nat! What would she tell her? What would she think? Had she come searching for Cat and seen them together? Was she looking for her still? What could she say? How on earth could she fix this? Cat was in the act of switching into high panic mode when she noticed a woman's hand on the Admiral's hip, one that was not her own.

She raised up on one elbow to see Natasha's eyes gleaming back at her, and the *rest* of the evening came flooding back.

"That was *FUN!*" whispered Nat, grinning, and clambered over the sleeping Marcus to cuddle behind her. Cat barely had time to feel the warmth of Nat down her spine before dropping, happily, into a dreamless sleep.

So in the closing days of the rafting, they became the Admiral's girls. Subject of much amusement, a bit of pride, and no small smattering of envy in the fleet. The rafting was even longer than anticipated. The weather held and the fleet held it's breath, fearing that the disaster would happen before they were ready and clear of the shallows, fearing that the Americans would finally decide to kill them all, not realizing that it would seal the doom of many thousands of their own citizens when the wave came, fearing the changes that were inevitably coming. By day, Cat and Natasha and Marcus ground away at the task, an endless cycle of conferences and meetings and simulations with an increasingly exhausted--albeit increasingly confident--crew. On the few days off, the three of them played at orgy, tumbling like children to blow off the stress. The years seemed to strip off of Marcus, and the sadness. He seemed not just in his element, he seemed himself again.

When the parting finally came, they kissed Marcus goodbye, tears pouring down their cheeks. The rafting planks were raised and dogged into place, the sails set, and the raft broken.

"How many things have changed." Said Natasha as they

swung the tiny Ganymeade to the northeast. "I would never have believed it."

Cat stood at the tiller of the little Weekender, the wind freshening and the water calm. Around them, a fleet of nearly two hundred small boats collected itself, all of them swinging to the north along the Gulf Stream. Nat embraced her from behind, warm skin against her, full of hope and trepidation, her great love, and now carrying--after much discussion--their child. Marcus' child. Cat's child. Sailing off to life and Armageddon.

How many things have changed, Cat thought. . .will change. . .and if you have the courage and are lucky, how fine a thing to finally become yourself.

28.   Cold Blooded Murder

Jas Silverman had been rather surprised when, on his return from the Fleet, he had been hailed as the Regime's leading authority on the "degenerates" of the seas. On his return, he had dutifully attended a debriefing in which he had carefully recounted all the things the President and his minions expected to hear. The Fleet was full of perverts, poverty widespread, lots of drug abuse, and that whole thing teetered on fracture and dissolution. All we have to do is wait, he told them, wait and then take credit for the soon to come fragmentation and disappearance of the Fleet. They ate it up.

So it was that when the post of Chief of Naval Operations opened, Silverman was the only name the Administration put forward to it's rubber stamp Congress. He was duly ensconced as the supreme naval authority of the Americas, a viper near the heart of the man his detractors already referred to as "The Emperor."

He had carefully suggested to the President that key officials, officers, pilots. . .all should be replaced with men who "could be trusted." What he failed to say was that the trust was all Admiral Silverman's, not the President's. Dutifully, key offices, pilots and crews of Air Force One and other official aircraft, even the helicopter crews serving the capitol were replaced with men of his choosing.

Jim Silverman bided his time. Indeed, time, for the first time in his life, seemed on *his* side for once. He had transferred to Washington, taking Capt. Kelly and most of his staff with him. He had a townhouse in Annapolis, went "fishing" on the weekends, and in general tried to blend in. Truth to tell, Silverman hated fishing. He knew the boat was his lifeline, the only way he was likely to survive the next year.

The Fleet had released its findings on the sea rise and the risk of a La Palma collapse that spring, to round derision from the White House. "Our research methods are superior," they trumpeted, "this is just fear mongering." Privately, though, the Administration that had built itself on fear had its doubts. So it was that Silverman, with Captain Kelly in tow, was summoned to Capitol Hill for a private briefing, to allay the fears of the powers that be, even if the official doctrine held that the environment could never be something to be feared.

Captain Kelly settled into the overstuffed chair the Pentagon had supplied them in an armored suite in the federal offices, settling into the gin and tonic Silverman had just poured him as well. Captain Spall, uncharacteristically, was stretched out on the inch thick carpet, relaxing. Ordinarily, the three of them would have had to pick their words carefully for fear of eavesdropping, but they were in charge now, surrounded by their own hand picked security people. It was surprisingly relaxing.

"What will you tell them?" asked Kelly.

Silverman settled in himself, leaning back with his drink on the ridiculously expensive leather couch. What opulence, he had thought, what stupidity.

"I'll tell them exactly what they want to hear. I'll tell them it's nonsense, that our research shows that nothing of the kind can happen. They'll spin it so hard they'll convince themselves it's true. I'll tell the President he should make a show of touring the eastern seaboard to show the Fleet and the Europeans that they're being ridiculous, and to show the world that only our research--and our interpretations--should be listened to. I'll tell him if there should, by some remote possibility, be a problem, we can always chopper them back to Camp David."

Spall looked at him quizzically.

"That doesn't make any sense, Jim."

Silverman smiled grimly to himself. He had been thinking about this for a long time.

"You're too young to remember this, David, but back in the Cold War days there was a huge competition for missile technology between America and the Russians....the old Soviet Union. . . "

"I'm not THAT young." said Spall.

"There was this general the Soviets had put in charge of new development. I forget his name. . ."Silvermann Continued, "they were working with some really dangerous fuels in an attempt to leapfrog ahead, hydrazine I think, and peroxide. His researchers were nervous. So at one test, to show it was safe, he put his chair *outside* the observation bunker to watch the launch. . ." he paused for effect.

"Go on" said Kelly, knowing the story. He liked it anyway.

"So of course all of his staff, the key researchers, party officials, anyone who wanted to suck up to him felt compelled to move their chairs out too, all of em, just to show that they were with the General."

"And?"

"And it blew. They all died. Every one of them."

There was a moment of silence. It took a second for Spall to get it.

"So you're expecting all the party functionaries, all the smarmy bastards who follow our dear and glorious leader, to accompany him on this great seaside photo op, right?" said Spall finally.

"You got it."

"And when the wave is actually on it's way. . . "

"And the roads are all jammed. . " chimed in Kelley.

"Then," said Silverman, "for some unknown reason, the

helicopters assigned to ferry the bastards to safer ground while everyone else drowns just never arrive."

"So what you're talking about is. . ."

"Cold blooded murder. . ." said Silverman, " yes."

They were all quiet for a moment.

"What about the people who live on the coast, " said Kelly finally, " What about them?"

"Who on earth, " said Captain Spall, " would believe that asshole when he says everything's safe? The minute he shows up on the coast, people will start to leave. They know him too well."

They all sat quietly after that, nursing their drinks. Later, Kelly would remark that it had been the first satisfying moment he'd felt in ages.

29.   Mare Sargassum

The Sargasso sea was another animal entirely from the Caribbean. There would be fewer days of sailing here, and month long raftings. There was no breeze for days at a time, and the humidity could be stultifying. Fishing boats had to go far afield, over to the Bermudas or up into arctic waters, just to find something to catch. Wind power didn't work well here, sail didn't work reliably here, and fuel consumption was at an all time high.

The preparations had gone well, and Cat was proud of them. The fish farms they'd brought, cages floating in the warm Sargasso filled water, were thriving, and the sargasso weed itself was a fine source of biofuel. Still, on one level, the fleet was like a giant volunteer organization, some folks flaking out, some dropping the ball, others overworked and overcommitted running with things often, it seemed, against the current. Was it like this, Cat wondered, in the early days of the fleet? A small village at sea, scrambling to meet their needs, scrambling to figure things out. . . .without the decades of Fleet experience behind them, she mused, it must've been overwhelming. She felt a new found and phenomenal respect for Carlin and Stephen and the original Fleet pioneers. As it was, the North Fleet was itself a mad scramble, flying on the edge of need and failure, and somehow, thank the gods of pirates, pulling it off.

The Americans, of course, had been delighted when the fleet had split. Someone, probably Marcus's friend Silverman, had given them the idea that this was some kind of schism, and word was circulating in the Federal press that the Northern Fleet were "fleeing the oppression of the Admiral and his minions." Word was they were negotiating sanctuary in Europe, or in Iceland. There were even tentative inquires from the Americans that riches could be theirs if they would just come to America and make a few public statements about the evils of the Fleet. Cat ignored them. The Americans, she reasoned, would find out why they were there soon enough, and the hard way.

So they came to the end of the first month in the Sargasso, and the very first Agoura of the Northern Fleet. Natasha had decked herself out in black, sexy despite the growing swell of her belly, or maybe because of it. Cat was in full 17th century gear, as was tradition, cutlass at her side. When the call came, she walked with her officers to the shaded agoura. The sea was flat, almost glassy. The air still, smelling of salt and seaweed.

The Agoura was set as was traditional, planks and benches, the Council in a semicircle around the officer's table. The Fleet's relic cutto was with the main body in the South Atlantic, but someone had substituted a glass box with a decayed Queen Anne flintlock in it's place, and there was a cannonball as gavel, and it occurred to Cat, she had never been here before, not like this, not as Admiral. She stood at the Officer's table before the Council, *her* Council. Every one of them, she knew. She looked at the crowd, large for an Agoura, looked at Nat's beaming face, looked at the seabirds over the Sargasso, flying hard in the still air. She knew how they felt. She swallowed hard, cleared her throat, lifted the rusting six pound shot, and struck it three times on it's monkey.

"Members of the council, by your orders we convene this meeting."

Silence. Not a word, not a motion. . .none of the Council sat. Everyone just stood there, hundreds of eyes on her.

Then the cheering began. It began with the Council, and then to Nat, and then to her Officers and then erupted all over the Agoura. They laughed and clapped and cheered til they were hoarse. Cat looked at the cannonball still in a deathgrip in her hand and began to laugh uncontrollably. Bottles appeared in the crowd, and wineskins and pipes and food, and the cheering went on. Hank, who had come along as her Constable, gave Cat a swat on the back that knocked her out of her rigid posture (and nearly off her feet). She turned to look at him with a move that came off to those assembled as a swagger, and the crowd roared even louder.

The party went on for a full ten minutes, and seemed unstoppable. But, with a wink to her beloved, Cat of **Ganymeade**, the Admiral of the Northern Fleet, brought brought her crew to order with a few swats of the cannonball on it's base, and so down to business.

30.   The Wave

The failure of the Greenland sheet was a slow motion
train wreck, beautiful and agonizing in its creeping,
inexorable pace. Strange striations appeared across
the satellite maps of the region, growing slowly, looking
for the world like creases in a white bedsheet. The
creases, though, were crevasses, parting gaps in the ice
down to bedrock, and the splitting continued. Thermal
photographs from space showed billions of gallons of icy
water flushing out from under the ice sheet into the
open sea. Fisheries were disrupted by the cold fresh
water. The Gulf Stream, the source of Northern
Europe's relatively balmy climate, became erratic.
Storms swept the region, freezing rains, high winds,
followed by bizarre periods of spring like warmth. Every
day, European tidal metrics showed the ocean levels
creeping up, millimetre by millimetre, while the
Americans decried "Old Europe's alarmism at what is a
natural, minor fluctuation in weather pattern."

On the raft of the Northern Fleet, day followed languid
day. Drills were held, fish were caught, dinners cooked
and eaten. . . .still the pressure was palpable. Tempers
began to flare. Arguments that would have turned into

sullen partings turned into open brawls. People were getting frayed.

To keep the lid on things, Cat began to create projects to keep the pressure and boredom from erupting. Her father had once told her that if people feel useless they make trouble for themselves. Cat and Natasha, along with old Stephen and some of the members of the constabulary had brainstormed all night, trying to come up with ways for people to participate, to be a part of the rescue and rebuild that was about to come, even before it happened.

So dozens of labor intensive projects swung into high gear. Fish were caught and dried or canned, seaweed was harvested and biofuel extracted. Water was purified and stored in cans and bottles and whatever else could be found. By the end of the month, there was nowhere left to store it all. Still, all the full larders and overtopped fuel tanks made the crew a bit more confident.

Amber came back from Bermuda with a new boyfriend, baskets of fresh food, and a firm treaty with the Bermudans for mutual aid. Knowing Amber, no one was surprised. Fleet mechanics helped ready the Bermudan fishing fleet for additional passengers, Bermuda filled the boats to brimming with fresh vegetables, corn and flour, and, of course, rum. Activity, some of it weirdly happy and oddly strained, was everywhere.

Still, the waiting continued. Crew members broke the monotony by brief vacations to St. George, many of them setting foot on land for the first time in years and staggering like drunks at first footfall on something that didn't MOVE.

Even Cat and Natasha managed a brief vacation or two,
touring the legendary caves and giggling and leaning on
each other like children, dining in unaccustomed
restaurants in front of a doting and amazed wait staff,
singing "Bully in the Alley" in Shinbone Alley at midnight.
. . . .it was a golden time, made all the sweeter
somehow by the hammer they knew was about to fall.

A month passed, two months. Cat had moored with the
raft from a three day circuit of the fleet, groggy and
dirty and yearning for bed, when her ansible chimed.
"You'd better get up here." said Hank from his post on
the monitoring ship **Willow**, "somethings. . . . ."

But she was already at a dead run.

The wave, when it came, was climax and anticlimax. It
was disaster. It was everyday. It was what they had
planned for, and more, and less.

The first clue came at three in the morning, when a call
from the astrophysical observatory on La Palma
indicated that something may be going on. It was the
last the station would be heard from. At about four, a
French satellite monitoring station confirmed that the
south face of the island had collapsed, and that a
tsunami was on it's way. The wave was about 500m
high and nearly 35 kilometers from crest to trough.
Forty minutes later, the seawater reached the
incandescent heart of Taburiente, the active volcano
that comprised the north half of La Palma, and the
island simply exploded. A second wave, moving even
faster, towering over 700m high and 60 kilometers
from crest to trough, would follow the first. The wave

height would, of course, decline with the square of the distance from the epicenter, but it would still be one hell of a wall of water when it reached them.

Through the early morning hours, the Fleet prepared, and was joined by boats from Bermuda, who had been kept appraised of the situation. They broke the raft at 8:30, turning their vessels to face the oncoming waves. It was probably a silly precaution, there being literally miles of water beneath them, but it at least felt like they were doing *something*. Calls were exchanged with the South Fleet. Cat and Natasha made a point of calling Marcus. He seemed calm and organized. His voice didn't sound unsteady until they told him they loved him. There were tears in his laughter. "Be careful." he said "Be safe."

A little before 10 AM a lookout with the fleet spotted the first wave. Cat was aboard **Maitland** with **Ganymeade** in tow, Cyndi handed her a hefty set of binoculars. It took her a moment to find the wave. It was so innocuous, and so very large. The wave appeared as a line on the horizon, a bulge in the ocean, no more. They held their breath. By the time the wave swept beneath them, though, it was barely apparent. There may have been a slight uplifting, a small sense of acceleration, and the sargasso was uncharacteristically turbulent. Other than that, nothing.

The second wave, now only half an hour behind, was more apparent, the lump on the horizon more pronounced. There was a definite rise this time, and Cat could make out the wave as it moved through the fleet. Still, in water this deep, the shockwave was no more than a boat wake, nothing to write home about.

"That was IT?" said Natasha, holding onto her from

behind.

Cat just nodded. "Give the order to raft again" she said to her Bosun "and tell Hank to let his Vespers and the rescue boats loose. They'll need em."

Cat turned and held Natasha to her for what seemed a very long time, just standing quietly, feeling her there. Then she kissed her softly and turned her attentions, and the **Maitland**, to the West and the grim work ahead.

31. Americans

Jas Silverman had gotten the word long before dawn,
and had piled Kelly and staff and families into two
black government vans and went racing north out of
Annapolis, heading for Hammock Island and his boat.
The lovely, sleepy little marina that was Hammock
Island was normally sail only, but the owners had
been happy to have a line on early warning, and
Silverman had given them a hefty bonus to moor his
massive powerboat there. The drive was not a
problem. All the traffic was headed the other way.
The word, somehow, was out already and the exodus
from the coast had begun.

Silverman had called ahead, and by the time he and
his entourage pounded across the bridge over to the
little island, most of the livaboards were already
raising sail. The marina's owners had gone from boat
to boat, rousing them. Silverman virtually leapt
aboard his sleek fishing boat, followed by Capt. Kelly
and the baggage. No one bothered to stow
anything. They just cast off. Jim Silverman turned the
key, cranked the throttle, and the roar of the boat's
twin V-8's startled a hundred seabirds from their
nests. By the time the sun rose, they would be safely
in deep water.

At Ocean City, the President was not having so lucky a time. The chain of command had become so politicized that no one wanted to tell the Commander in Chief that the impossible had, indeed, taken place, and that the wave that couldn't happen was on it's way. It was nearly eight before the President was dragged dripping from his shower with the news.

An area in the parking lot was cleared and the Marine helicopters were summoned to lift them to safety. Helicopters which, oddly, never arrived. A panicked call from Hilton Head island revealed that the Vice President, on his own leg of the Administration's Coastal Tour to the south, was having the same problem.

Secretary of Defense Ginwold, traveling with his Commander in Chief, tired of the dithering. He took charge, placing calls to area military bases, themselves in the midst of their own evacuations. Strangely his calls were diverted, dropped, or simply ignored. It didn't take him long to figure it out.

"Silverman, you fucking son of a bitch." he snapped to no one in particular.

Still, the Secretary was far from done. He instructed his staff to call the President's corporate allies for help. But the corporate jets were busy ferrying corporate presidents and their families to safety. After nearly an hour of desperate calls, he managed to line up a number of news helicopters and the transit choppers of two rich churches allied to the President.

But when the choppers landed, security was inadequate. The crowd had rushed them, actually tipping one of them over before the blades had stopped, and the attendant carnage only made the chaos worse. One of the news choppers managed to make it to safety, mostly packed with reporters and security guards. Another transit chopper lurched airborne with two Senators and the Secretary of Commerce, but the replacement pilot--the original one having been trampled to death by the mob--hadn't been in the cockpit since the second Iraq war, failed to account for winds between the tall hotel buildings, and slammed the aircraft into the rotating restaurant atop a Holiday Inn.

And that was that.

The wave, when it came, was astonishing. The second, faster wave had by this time caught up with its slower little brother, and the resulting wall of water, stacked high by climbing the continental shelf, was over 200 metres high and moving at over 400 kilometers an hour. It came up from the horizon with astonishing speed, a wall the height of an office tower, with the noise of a hundred thousand freight trains.

Secretary Ginwold stood on the balcony of one of the beachfront hotels, resigned to what was about to happen. He was, for all his faults, at least a man of some dignity. He turned to his President, the man who he had followed to power and now to destruction, wanting desperately to say something, wanting desperately to hear some word of closure.

The President, the "Captain of the Free World," was leaning on the railing a few feet from him. The President had been through phases of shouting, crying, and howling already this morning. Now he was merely staring out at the water, out at the wave, trembling uncontrollably.

"Mister President?" Ginwold shouted over the roar. The President turned to him, mouth agape, eyes with a deer-in-the-headlights glaze. Ginwold noted, bitterly, that his President, the "Captain of the Free World," had soiled himself.

"You pathetic Fuck." said Ginwold, though no one could hear him over the noise.

It wasn't much in the way of last words, anyway.

32. Aftermath

It happened as Marcus had predicted it would.
Heading west, the Vespers had first encountered a
wave of refugees, small boats all fleeing the wave
and the destruction. Some were swamped, others
horribly overloaded, some with passengers still in
pajamas, some filled with sick and dying that their
skippers had pulled from the roiling, polluted waters
by the coast. The Patrol did what it could, pointing
them toward the raft, treating emergencies, and in
general trying to convince the refugees that the ports
they had left were no longer there, that the seas
would likely not recede from the ruined coast for
centuries, and that they were lucky to be breathing
and dry.

Then came a wave of derelict vessels, some broken
free from moorings, some floated off of trailers and
boatel storage racks. Some were huge cargo ships,
listing precariously, dead in the waters. Some were
tiny rowboats and sailboats, rigged as though for an
outing. Some were pristine, fully stocked, as though
the skipper had just stepped overboard on a calm
day and vanished. Others were swamped, holed,
ruined. Those that could be saved were towed back
to the raft, long trains of vessels in the still water

tugged by a straining Vesper or recovered powerboat. The others were stripped and sunk so they wouldn't endanger navigation.

Then was the flotsam. Roofs of buildings, great tangles of telephone poles and wire, mattresses and coolers and cars and anything else that would float and that the sea could get its grips on. There were steel shipping containers by the thousands, some riding high, others barely submerged, a threat to even the shallow draught Vespers. There was plastic everywhere, bottles and shards of foam insulation and children's toys.

Then there were the bodies. Men and women and children and cats and dogs and livestock, all of them beaten and scarred by being ground by the waves of debris. There were unidentifiable lumps of what had to have been some kind of flesh. There were disconnected limbs. And occasionally, just occasionally, there were survivors. An old man, shivering in the water, would call out to them. A pretty little girl, dry and astonishingly clean, perched atop a floating roof, calling for her mommy. A sick woman, bleeding and unconscious, holding onto her dead child atop a raft of debris and furniture. . . .

Reaching the new coastline was impossible. The skeletons of ruined buildings stood up out of the seas at what had been the shore, a shore that would not feel the touch of dry air again for centuries. Locked between these was a layer of debris that had been ripped from the land, in some places tens of meters thick. You'd have a better chance walking than sailing to the new coast, they said.

So they rescued the rescuable, treated the ill. They took from the bodies that had them wallets and rings and ID bracelets and entered the names or what information they found into an internet list, a "Necronomicon" old Stephen had grimly put it, the names of those dead. They popped the locks on the shipping containers, salvaged what was usable, and filled them with the corpses of men and animals, slammed them shut, holed them, and sent them to the bottom so that the sea might deal with those it had taken in a sanitary fashion.

A feed from a Russian satellite, forwarded to them by the EU, told some of the tale of changes. North America was beyond recognition, the southern states submerged beneath a shallow sea, the continent divided by a narrow gulf that once had been the Mississippi river valley. Central Europe was aflood, the whole middle of China a shallow estuary, filled with debris and millions of dead. From Marcus they learned that the shining cities of Venezuela and Surinam were gone. That at the port of Rio the waves had struck with such velocity that the statue of Christ was ripped from his mountain top and the shattered trunk now stood atop a bare island in what was once the harbor.

Closer to home, the Bermudans returned to find that only Town Hill, scoured clean by the waves, remained above the waters. Some returned to England or Canada. Most joined the fleet. The with the refugees, the population of the North Fleet would hit 53,000, the South Fleet nearly half a million. Expeditions to the Indian and Pacific oceans started the formation of native fleets there. By the end of two years, there would be three million living on the water, but that's another story.

The Patrol had brought to their Admiral a derelict

Bolger AS 49 called the **Aphrodite**, immaculately kept and built lovingly by an elderly man on the Eastern Shore who was now, doubtless, part of the flotsam ringing America. Cat was glad to have it. The spacious salon of the big sharpie was a much better place to hold meetings, and besides, with the baby coming, they would need more room than the little cabin of the **Ganymeade**. So in the midst of everything else, she and Nat had moved in, keeping **Ganymeade** as a tender. One day, she decided, **Ganymeade** would be their child's first vessel. A family legacy. Who would have figured?

So it was that some three months after the wave, Cat found herself sitting in **Aphrodite**'s cavernous salon, looking across a table strewn with charts at Jas Silverman. Silverman had returned to take command of the surviving eastern fleet of the U.S., had overseen rescue operations, had dispatched arctic icebreakers into what had been the Chesapeake and New York harbor to break through the debris and open a way to what would become new ports for the Continent. As always, he had done his work with competence and tirelessness. At year's end, though, he had announced his intention to retire. He would hand off the tiller of command to younger sailors he could trust, would retire to the fleet, and, like his old friend Marcus, sign the Articles. Cat was pleased.

"I think my leg's asleep." Said Silverman, gently shifting Cyndi of **Maitland** off his lap. The two of them had been an item since he first set foot on the raft after the wave, and the both of them looked better for it.

"You think I'm fat." she said, pouting.

"I think you're heavy," Jim said, grinning, "that's

different."

Cat didn't know Silverman well, but mused that it just seemed *right* to see him playful. She could see how he and Marcus could have gotten along.

At that point Capt. Kelly came down the ladder with a sheaf of papers and rom cards, fresh from the communications room of the U.S.S. Amberjack, the massive destroyer which was now moored incongruously alongside the much smaller vessels of the raft. He dumped them on the table.

"There's the projections..." he said "or what there is of them."

"Give us a summary." Cat and Silverman said in unison, then looked at each other a bit startled.

"Great" said Kelly, "two Admirals, no waiting." and laughed. Sometimes Cat and Silverman were waaay too much alike, and it unnerved him occasionally. Must be an Admiral thing.

"First of all, with the Gulf Stream and the Atlantic Current disrupted, it's gonna get fuck-all cold in the north this winter. Europe is gonna freeze. Nova Scotia as well. This may go on for four to six years until the warmer current reestablishes itself."

"Enough to drop some of the sea levels?" asked Cat. Silverman looked at her respectfully. He hadn't thought of that.

"Not meaningfully." said Kelly, "and then there will be a temperature spike. All of this floating crap is rotting and releasing methane and CO_2. It'll restart warming until plant media and the currents can start sequestering again. Beyond that, it's hard to say. Too many variables."

"Chaos theory." said Cyndi. Higher math was her hobby. "Gotta love it."

"There were three computers on the planet that could have tackled simulations on this, and two of them are under water at the moment." continued Kelly. "the Japanese are crunching away at it, but their's wasn't as fast as the one in Virginia Beach, and their OS is . . .well. . .cumbersome by comparsion. We hope by the end of the month. . . ."

"Jim, the refugees that want to go back to the mainland should be able to by. . .what. . .middle of next month?" asked Cat.

He nodded. "We've got three ports open and functioning now, and supplies really aren't an issue. We've got tons of consumer goods that now have no where to go and no one living to feed. We already have reception and housing centers set up at two of em."

"So we'll plan on sending them home by summer's end. The rest of us will head south around the middle of October before the winter hits and try to establish a new cycle pattern. The Southern Fleet is staying off the African Coast for the time being--they need access to food supplies for the refugees--so we're on our own in the Caribbean for the foreseeable future. There'll be plenty of maneuvering room. There's only Cuba, Hispaniola, Jamaica, and a few of the Windwards left above water, and I've no idea at all what the circulation pattern is going to look like."

"The simulations will help with that when we get them," said Kelly, "but whether or not they'll actually pan out to be true is anyone's guess."

Cyndi let out a long sigh. "Is it 5:00 O'Clock yet?"

"It's always 5:00 O'Clock somewhere." Silverman and Cat said in unison. It was one of Marcus' favorite phrases.

"You two, " said Kelly, "are fucking freaking me out." and he headed for the spirits locker.

33. The Ganymeade Protocol

That evening, right at sunset, the air was warm and gentle, and there was, for a change, a hint of a breeze. The sunset was unusually beautiful, reds and oranges scattered across the Western sky.

Red sky at night, sailor's delight.

Cat sat on the rail of the **Aphrodite**, wine glass in one hand, Natasha on the seat between her knees, cradling her growing belly and drowsing as Cat stroked her dark hair. Somewhere, someone was playing a guitar, and there were voices singing in harmony, a Chanty, something old. There was the sound of children. Someone was barbecuing. There were the cries of seabirds and the incessant music of halyards as the boats rolled softly in the mild sea.

Her father had called it "the Ganymeade Protocol:" a set of rules for living on the ocean that he had set down the day they had launched **Ganymeade** into the bay for the first time. "Number One, "he'd said, "respect the ocean as a living thing, and live with it as a friend. You'll stay alive a lot longer that way. Number two, greet each coming day--however challenging it looks--as an opportunity to be better and happier, and you will be. Number three, embrace change, embrace the new like a child getting a new toy. Look forward to it, even if you didn't choose it. And last," he'd said "keep those you love, those who love you, close by. Do this, Katie, and I promise, you'll be safe and you'll be happy."

And somewhere in that glorious sunset, with Natasha's cheek warm on her thigh and surrounded by the fleet, her home. . .somewhere in the music of seabird and halyard, she thought she heard the faint warm sound of his laughter, and a voice that said:

"Katie, love, I told you so."

About the Author

Dr. Don Elwell is a playwright, director, actor, and teacher, founder of both the Greylight Theatre and Grindlebone Arts theatre companies. He grew up sailing the warm waters of the northern Gulf of Mexico before turning to a long and successful career as theatrical artist and writer. He is the author of the "Coyote" trilogy of plays (*Coyote, Cyberpunk Opera,* and *Dub for Babylon*) as well as the short novel "In The Shade" and a number of other works. He currently directs and teaches in Pennsylvania.